THE PENDANT

Between Worlds

Book Three

Books by Cynthia Austin

The Pendant Series
Book One: Between Dreams
Book Two: Between Loves
Book Three: Between Worlds

**Coming Soon!
The Pendant Series**
Book Four: Between Life
Book Five: Between Death

**For more information
visit:** www.SpeakingVolumes.us

THE PENDANT

Between Worlds

Book Three

Cynthia Austin

SPEAKING VOLUMES, LLC
NAPLES, FLORIDA
2024

Between Worlds

Copyright © 2015 by Cynthia Austin

All rights reserved. No part of this book may be reproduced or transmitted in any form or by any means without written permission.

This book is a work of fiction. The names of characters, places, and incidents are products of the author's imagination and are not to be construed as real. Any resemblance to persons, living or dead, actual events, locale or organizations is entirely coincidental.

ISBN 979-8-89022-118-6

To Mom
Thank you for everything.

Acknowledgments

Thank you to the dedicated readers that have encouraged me to continue writing this series. Your support means the world to me.

A big thank you to my author support team, Racheal Tamayo and Andrea Roche. Always knowing I can come to you ladies for any bit of writing advice is amazing.

Last, a big thank you to Kurt and Erica at Speaking Volumes. Without your faith, the next two installments may never have made it past the scribbles on my laptop.

Chapter One

Little Devotional

I stood on his porch, drenched in rain water as I pounded on the big red door. I should have felt silly, showing up unannounced in the middle of the night, but I was too desperate to allow myself to feel anything other than the way I did.

The porch light flicked on, and I saw him peek out the window at me. His eyes looked sleepy, and I knew I had awoken him.

He opened the door wearing only a pair of dark gray sweatpants and I realized the instant I felt my breath catch that it was the first time I'd ever seen him without a shirt. Although Adrian was on the thin side, he still had the toned body of an athlete.

I opened my mouth to speak. I was eager to explain my marriage proposal from Ray and I was anxious for him to give me the friendly advice that he had so often shared. Instead, I mutely stood there, staring at his six pack abs.

He looked me up and down, but instead of a smile, his eyes met mine and they held nothing but disappointment. I remained frozen in place, soaking wet, wearing the blue cocktail dress. The look in my eyes was the saddest part of my appearance.

He knew.

"You went to see him." It wasn't a question but more of a statement. A statement which allowed me to see the feelings of hurt and betrayal written all over his face.

Since it wasn't a question, I didn't feel the need to answer.

He folded his arms and stood in the doorway, not inviting me inside. Instead, he used his body as a barricade and forced me to remain outside in the cold. As I shivered, he mocked my decision.

"What'd he do to you this time?"

"Nothing," I whispered. "It was perfect. *He* was perfect."

Adrian grimaced at my response and placed his hand on his hip as he shook his head. "Well, if everything was so perfect, why are you here? Shouldn't you be living the Hollywood dream somewhere else, like say . . . in Hollywood?"

He started to close the door but I put my hand against the painted wood. My intentions in going to his house tonight were pure, but my actions and words deceived me. More importantly, they were deceiving Ray. I began rethinking my decision to run to Adrian.

Why was I here?

Standing drenched, with the dress clinging to my body and my beautiful curls now clumps of tangles, I stared into Adrian's eyes, silently begging for him to understand my presence on his porch without making me say it aloud. He wasn't budging and I knew my window for rebuttal was small. I needed to speak fast before he shut the door in my face forever.

"Why are you here, Sidney?" he asked again though gritted teeth.

"Because you're my Gatsby, Adrian," I blurted out. "I was with Ray all night and while everything was perfect, I couldn't stop thinking about you. Because you're my Gatsby."

Adrian froze.

He wasn't expecting that response. I pounced on the element of surprise, spouting off before the courage evaporated as quickly as it arrived.

"You told me you hadn't kissed me because I hadn't figured it out yet. Well, I have figured it out, so what's stopping you now?"

I pressed against the door and this time Adrian allowed it to open further.

"I've spent every day with you these past few months. I know you feel the same way about me as I do for you. So why haven't you kissed me?"

I took a step closer, but he backed up as if I were a rabid dog.

"Don't," was all he said.

I crossed the threshold and entered the big white house and this time Adrian stayed in place. I gripped the hem of his sweatpants so he couldn't get away from me and looked into his green eyes.

Those pendant eyes.

My pendant eyes.

There was a hunger inside of them but there was also a flicker of sadness he was unable to hide from me. He dropped his gaze to my necklace. Reaching his hand up and twirling the emerald stone in his fingers, he refused to look at me.

I refused to accept his diversion.

I wrapped my hand around his, forcing his attention back to me.

"You're so busy using Ray as an excuse, but I think it's because you're still in love with *her*," I pressed, referring to his lost love who shared the same necklace. This time as Adrian held my gaze I refused to look away. I would rather melt into nothingness than break away from his stare.

"I see the pain in your eyes every time you look at my necklace. I won't hurt you the way she hurt you, Adrian. I won't leave you."

It was as if I were possessed and the words that flowed out of my mouth were not my own. They may have been words I had always wanted to say to Adrian, but I'd never had the confidence to actually get them out.

Not a problem now.

His bare chest was so close to me, I could feel the heat radiating off of his body. I could hear his accelerated breathing. It dramatically changed when I had gotten close to him.

He gasped, "I won't be able to stop myself."

I was confused. "Pardon?"

"Once I kiss you, I won't be able to stop myself," he clarified.

I took a step closer, this time moving my hands from the waist of his sweats and brushing them across his washboard abs. He was smaller than Ray but just as muscular. I gripped the sides of his waist with both hands ensuring that he wouldn't escape me. I closed my eyes and summoned the courage inside me to not back out now. I had wanted this for so long and now it seemed he was willing to comply. Our bodies were now touching. It wasn't possible to get any closer than this. His breathing intensified and I could feel his hot breath on my neck. There was nothing in this world I wanted more at that moment than his lips on mine.

Finally, his body responded, and he gripped both of my arms and held me close to him, but it wasn't an embrace. It was more like a warning. One last chance to flee.

"Don't do this unless you mean it, Sidney. I don't play games."

My heart was on fire. "I do mean it."

His voice was husky now. "Every time I get close to you, you run away."

"That was the old Sidney. I'm not going to run away anymore," I assured him.

He moved my body backwards as I retreated against the foyer wall. His right hand shot up, trapping me. My entire being, emotionally, psychologically, and physically, was now checkmated. He was testing me. He was making sure I had nowhere to run.

I turned my head to the side and closed my eyes. I could feel his breath on my cheek. He was that close to me.

Breathe, Sidney. Just breathe.

Then, as if he wasn't close enough already, he took another step toward me, so our bodies were intimately touching all the way down.

He needed to hear this. "I'm not fighting it anymore. I've wanted you since the first day we met."

Those words were all it took to have his lips on mine.

And his lips were all I needed to make me realize what I had known all along.

I could fall deeper with Adrian than I had ever fallen with Ray. This much I knew was true, but in order to do so I had to let go of Ray, and even though I was here with Adrian, getting lost in the moment, I wasn't sure if I was ready to do that. Even as we kissed I was conflicted between the two men; one I had always loved, and the other I was ready to love.

Ray always came back to me, but Adrian had never left me to begin with. When the day ended he was still with me. I had to choose.

Now.

Forcing the thought of Ray out of my mind, I focused only on Adrian and allowed myself to get lost in the moment I had dreamt about for months. His mouth was like a stove, and every time it touched my body it sent my blood into a boil. Somehow we bypassed the foyer, and I ended up pressed against the wall at the bottom of the staircase. Adrian broke away from our kiss and gripped my face with both of his hands as he stared intently into my eyes. "Your heart may be broken now but if you let me, I'll fix it. I'll give you mine."

I closed my eyes and allowed the words to sink into my brain. No one had ever been this committed to me; I felt if I let him, Adrian could be my everything.

He really was my prince.

"I have this version of you in my mind," I began. "This version of some perfect guy who knows me better than I know myself, this man who's incapable of hurting me. Don't destroy my dream. Don't let me down."

Adrian kissed me long and hard. "As long as you stay with me you'll have nothing to fear."

I didn't know if that was meant to be a threat or a reassurance of his feelings for me. Whatever it was, it sent shivers down my spine all the way to my feet.

"What song's playing in your mind right now?" he breathed.

Without missing a beat, I replied by naming one from his very own playlist. "That Marilyn Manson song, 'Evidence.'"

Adrian's lips curved up into a delicious smile as he recalled that tune. "You know that song is a huge warning. It's got nothing but red flags sounding through it."

Still struggling to catch my breath I nodded my head in agreement, silently screaming at the room to stop spinning. "The warnings are going off in my head right now."

Adrian held my gaze, unwavering. "What are you going to do about it?"

Refusing to look away, I promised, "Ignore them."

"That's probably a bad idea."

Before I could respond, Adrian's lips were once again on mine as he pressed me into the staircase wall with his body.

The warning bells rang out louder now.

This was all happening too fast. There's only one thing that could happen if I stay here. I need to leave. Now!

At that point, Adrian confirmed my suspicion as he gripped the bottom of my dress and slowly began to inch it up my legs.

"What are you doing?" I gasped.

He answered with a kiss. He pressed his body firmly against me and kissed me deeper. My thoughts began to swirl as I gave in to the kiss I had been waiting for the past six months. I hadn't realized how often I'd thought about it until it was actually happening, and it far exceeded my expectations.

Breaking away and leaving us both breathless, he flashed me a sexy smile and seductively answered, "We're both adults here. I think you know what comes next."

And I did know. I just couldn't believe it was happening. Things were rolling along too quickly here. I had only come here to declare my revelation concerning my feelings for him.

There was a new agenda now.

Placing his lips back on mine he slowly worked to make me lose my reserve. The voice of reason became nothing more than a muffled sound as I accepted my fate with Adrian. My hands effortlessly swept over every inch of him, as if his body was second nature to me. All second thoughts flew out of my head as I closed my eyes and reminded myself to live for the moment.

That was what I'd been doing for the past six months. With the absence of Ray came the absence of my identity. I had spent so many years wound up in the world of *his* dream that I had forgotten what it was like to live for myself.

Everything was so bleak after he'd left me that looking into the future seemed to be as impossible as establishing world peace. I counted it a small victory just to get through the next 24 hours, constantly reminding myself to live only in the moment. And now that moment seemed to be making out with Adrian in the staircase of his dead relative's house.

"Do you want to go upstairs?"

"Okay," I meekly replied before he lifted me up and carried me up to his bedroom. We fell onto the gray satin sheets and continued where we'd left off . . .

Living in the moment.

And in one instant he went from being Adrian, my loyal friend who was there to piece me back together each and every time Ray destroyed me; to being Adrian, a man who was completely in control of my body and now possessed the ability to make me lose myself in him.

We made love. It was perfect.

Chapter Two

To the End

The bedroom was covered in dark patterned wallpaper with equally dark curtains and bedding to complement the space. There were two large floor-to-ceiling windows with panels on each side. The walnut-colored bamboo floors were scuffed with age. I noticed all of this stuff as I silently lay in Adrian's bed safely protected in his arms.

What a feeling!

In a way, the room fit what my imagination had always pictured the inside of the McAllister house to be; dark and creepy, but somehow Adrian also managed to give it a look of classic Old-World charm.

Turning to face him, I gripped his neck and snuggled into his chest. I was on Cloud Nine and never wanting to come back down. Adrian cupped my chin, tilting my face up as he plucked a kiss from my lips. Then we just lay there, staring at each other with the help of the hallway light illuminating through the cracked bedroom door.

I loved looking into his vibrant green eyes, searching for the thoughts buried deep within them. He was hard to read, but I still enjoyed trying.

"That was interesting," I said.

"You're welcome," he answered, never moving his eyes from mine.

I brought the sheet over my head and covered my beet red face. He was the sexiest human being alive. "And what is it exactly that I should be thankful for, Mr. McAllister?"

"Me, for helping you to finally open your eyes."

His response kind of threw me as the words sent me crashing back into reality and with it came the memory of Ray's proposal only hours before.

"Actually . . . I think I could see better before. It's kind of dark in this bedroom," I joked, trying to see only the humor in this.

I was having trouble accepting what I had just done to Ray.

Of course, Adrian didn't find my comment amusing at all. With a very serious expression on his face, he stared into my eyes before finally breaking the silence. "Sidney, what if I told you I really wasn't here right now, that you summoned me to you somehow. Would that make sense to you?"

Did he really just ask that?

Now I was thankful for the blanket of darkness. I didn't want Adrian to see the struggle it took to gulp down the nervous lump in my throat but I'm sure he could hear it. I had never told Adrian about my dreams, and furthermore, I never intended to; unless I wanted him to make a call and send me to the loony bin.

But now with him asking such a direct question, it almost seemed as if he'd known I'd actually dreamt him up before meeting him.

"Like, I created you? That would be crazy, Adrian," I scoffed, hiding my nervousness. "I can touch you so you *are* really here." Reaching out, I traced my fingertips lightly down the hard curves of his chest. I continued to try and make us real. "I can kiss you," I said, a little softer as I leaned down and brushed my lips against his.

Instead of closing my eyes and getting lost in the kiss, I looked at his face. He was so perfect. Complementing his oval countenance were those big green eyes with long, thick lashes that encased them, and a small heart-shaped mouth.

I was mystified how all of his teeth fit into that sexy, tiny mouth of his. He pulled me closer and I swear my heart stopped the instant his lips touched mine.

"How are you so perfect?" The words came out before I could stop them.

He just smiled, like there was some joke only he knew.

"See, you created me. I am the Mona Lisa of your mind."

"You're so weird!" I laughed as I gave him a playful shove. He gripped my wrist and pulled me in for another kiss. This was a much more serious kiss which caused all of the humor to be sucked right out of the room.

When I pulled away I felt him inhale sharply. I could feel his breath against my cheek. He smelled like mint and lemon water. Amazingly there was no trace of nicotine.

"What if I told you I loved you?" he whispered.

I could handle that a lot easier than I could handle his suggestion of him merely being a delusion.

Lost in the moment, I so foolishly repeated those words to him. "I love you too." I may have meant them. It *felt* like I meant them when I said it. But it didn't change the fact that I also loved Ray. My heart was so screwed up.

And Adrian had no idea.

Closing my eyes as I rested my head on Adrian's chest, I listened to the calming rhythm of his heart beating until sleep finally surrounded me.

Chapter Three

Attack

When I opened my eyes I was in the place I'd often dreamt of many times before. I sat up and looked around. Somehow, it seemed different this time. As if everything was much clearer in vision and texture.

It seemed as if I'd looked at the scene through a dirty mirror before and now the mirror was sparkling clean. For the first time, I could smell the beauty of it all and see every detail. I took an invigorating breath and laughed out loud when I realized I could actually smell the scent of sweet jasmine flowers. Before, I was nothing but a spectator in this other world, but now I was a part of it. I gazed up and admired the blue sky full of puffy white clouds. I felt the sun beating down on my bare arms, radiating its heat into my skin. It was like everything was in 3-D. It was exhilarating.

The scenery seemed to stretch for miles; row upon row of corn and wheat fields with line after line of perfectly placed fruit trees. The untouched earth beneath me had all sorts of stunning wildflowers sprouting from the dirt. Deep back behind the cornfield was a wall of eucalyptus trees, their heavy leaves swaying back and forth in the wind.

Golden hills swallowed up the entire valley, giving me a sense of serenity. The land reminded me of my childhood when I had been as free as a soaring eagle to explore the undeveloped areas of my neighborhood. That same sense of freedom was here with me now.

Suddenly I saw a giant shadow cast upon my face as a figure stood in front of me and held out his oversized hand to me. I was baffled. In all the times I'd visited this place, no one had ever been able to see me.

Until now.

I took his hand without hesitation. It was warm and welcoming. The sun blazed behind him, darkening his figure and allowing the rays of sunlight to beam off his body. The bright light made it impossible for me to see the details of his face other than a shadow profile of a man, but I could feel his peaceful aura and knew he was here only to help me.

As I stood up, the sun sank below him, and with the glare out of my eyes, I could now see him clearly, and I gasped at the sight.

Immediately, I retracted my hand from his grip. "I know you. You're Samael's father."

His voice boomed, "I am. In a way, I am everyone's Father. At least I like to look at myself in that eternal sense."

I snorted at his arrogance.

He lowered his voice. "I've brought you here to warn you."

I folded my arms and looked at him in disbelief. "Warn me?"

"He's not as he appears, Sidney."

Didn't my mother say the same thing?

I was afraid to say his name. "S-Samael?"

"You know him as Adrian," said the shadow Father.

I was stupefied, and suddenly scared. "They're the same person? How is that even possible?"

"The Devil wears many faces."

His answer was as shocking as a slap to my face. I may have not been the most religious person in the world, but I did know of the Devil and Adrian was far from the monstrous villain humanity had painted Satan out to be.

Besides, the Devil existed as much as God did and I wasn't sure I believed in either one. I sputtered out a response. "Why would you say that?"

Samael's father stood erect, arms folded as he gazed into the distance, staring at nothing in particular. Then he turned and his next words sent a chill through me. "He's an evil one, that child of mine; both he and his sister. Death has followed them ever since they exited their mother's womb only seconds apart."

My head was spinning with confusion. I was trying to wrap my mind around this information that had slammed my senses into a wall of stone. There was no way I could accept what this man was saying to me. Adrian wasn't evil and he didn't even have a sister. No, this was all wrong. Adrian was not Samael or the Devil or any of those things.

He is my friend . . . and maybe my lover.

I stood up verbally to the giant figure looming over me. "You've got to be mistaken. Adrian is not Samael."

I took a step back. I felt my instinct to run beginning to kick in as I visually scoured the land, seeking out the quickest escape route. But being unfamiliar with the land, I had no idea where to go. Besides, if this guy was truly God, where could I go?

Panic was setting in. "This is not real right now . . . this is a dream!"

I pinched my arm, forcing myself to wake up from this nightmare. But Samael's father continued to speak as if he had not even heard my scream.

"Her poor body could not withstand their torment. She died moments after giving them life."

I put my hands up to my ears, refusing to allow these lies to enter my brain. "Adrian doesn't have a twin sister! No, you must be confused. Adrian's mother did not die during childbirth. His parents died together last year in a car accident," *I shrieked, begging him to acknowledge he'd made a mistake.*

But he wouldn't budge. His eyes were hard and emotionless. There was no give and take in his manner. He wouldn't accept my version of the story.

"Everything out of my son's mouth is deceit. He'll twist your vision of things until it's an ugly distorted mess. He's already gotten his claws into you. You've allowed yourself to question your judgment of what you know to be right. With the help of his evil sister, he's been able to get you to push away everything good in your life."

"Sister?"

That one word was all it took to send the memories of my last dream crashing into my brain. Just as clear as my dream was now, apparently so were my memories. And as the memory of the inappropriate sibling dream flooded my brain so did the images of Lilly and Adrian.

"That's impossible," *I whispered. I shot the old man a revolting look.* "You're doing this to me! You're putting these images in my mind. You're the one trying to make me believe things that aren't real!"

"You've lost your faith, Sidney," *he replied with a calm reverence.*

Now I felt nothing but anger. This man had to be tricking me, distorting my memories to see facts that weren't real. Adrian and Lilly didn't even know each other. This whole thing was ludicrous. I fought back. "Faith in what . . . faith in God?" *I snorted.* "I never had faith in something I couldn't see."

"Look around you, Sidney. What do you see? Where are you?"

I closed my eyes, refusing to comply with his request and instead willed myself to wake up. "I'm dreaming," *I said through gritted teeth.*

Wake up, Sidney. Open your eyes!

I could almost feel my heavily sedated body back in the other world. I closed my eyes and tried hard to make that Sidney lift her arm or turn her head. I tried to make her move something that would jolt her back into consciousness.

But it was no use.

The impudent man would not stop his torture. "Why the same dream? Why is your dream written in Adrian's book? Why does it correlate with a religious book if religion is not real? Who is Adrian and what does he want from you? That's what you need to ask yourself. If you can answer that question you will be freed from your torment."

Finally, the connection from my brain to my nerves seemed to plug back in and with a spark, I could move my arm. I flopped myself so hard my entire body came crashing off Adrian's bed and hit hard against the wooden floor. My eyes shot open. I was finally awake, but those final words lingered in my brain.

Freed from my torment . . . what torment?

Awake and alert, I looked about the unfamiliar room and all at once the memories of last night came rushing into my head.

Denying what my memories screamed to me, I reached over and grabbed my blue dress, hugging it tightly.

Shit, Sidney. You've really made a mess of things now.

I curse inwardly to myself as I quietly collected my belongings from all over Adrian's bedroom. How could I have let this happen? Why couldn't this have happened yesterday *before* I had received Ray's package? So much could have changed in that short span of time. Now it was too late.

I had wanted Adrian for months, so much so I finally found the courage to call him out on it and what had he done? He had shut me down. Then, the instant Ray came back into my life he finally unloaded his feelings and made me his lover.

I glanced angrily at Adrian, who was still sleeping soundly in the bed. But once I saw his peaceful face, I could no longer pass the blame on to him. This was my mess. He was just a casualty of Ray's and my war. Images of last night kept playing in my mind. Our kisses, caresses, and the words we said reverberated in my mind.

Stupid. Stupid. Stupid.

I closed my eyes and willed the memories away. Last night, in the heat of the moment, Adrian said he loved me. And like a big idiot I told him I loved him too. This was not a total lie, but a lie just the same. Yes, I did love Adrian, but I loved Ray too. Ray asked me to marry him last night.

What was I going to do *today*?

Not wanting to answer that question, I continued searching the room, reassembling my wardrobe by picking up my scattered articles of clothing. This was not helping erase the memories of our erotic night together. I dressed as quickly and silently as I could. Then, I began the hunt for my shoes. I think they fell off somewhere mid-stairs while Adrian was carrying me up to his bedroom . . .

Shaking my head, I grabbed my purse and exited the room.

One heel lay just where I suspected, but the other was still a mystery. Tip-toeing down the wooden stairs, I felt like Cinderella searching for the missing slipper.

But if I was Cinderella, who was my Prince?

I saw it lying in front of the double doors to the library. I scooped up the shoe and in a flash I was at the big red door and ready to fly away.

But something stopped me from taking another step. I turned back around and headed deeper into the McAllister mansion.

Chapter Four

Tightrope

I found myself standing in front of the doors to the enormous study.

The library was, far and away, my favorite room in the McAllister house. This was not surprising since the room was so fascinating. It was the centerpiece for the tours that used to take place years ago.

Putting my heel back on my foot, I debated abruptly leaving before Adrian woke up to avoid that awkward morning after a night of sex talk. The one where we both would futilely try to read each other's body language in the hopes of finding out if last night's escapade meant as much as it did to the other person.

I'd just as soon leave and let Adrian conclude it didn't mean a thing to either of us. It was simply a mistake. I was sure he knew it too. But just as I turned to exit the house, a sense of déjà vu enveloped me as I remembered the odd dream I had just experienced. It was a phrase that rendered me frozen in my tracks.

Why is your dream written in Adrian's book?

That's what Samael's Father had asked me. I racked my brain for the meaning behind his words. Then I remembered the night of Ray's arrest. After our fight, I had run back to Adrian's house. He was in the library arguing with a client on the phone while searching for something. I opened the doors to the library and quietly crept forward as I recalled that night.

There had been a safe hidden behind one of the bookcases. I'd watched as Adrian slid the bookcase away from the wall and revealed it.

But what had been in that safe?

I closed my eyes and focused on that night. I was an emotional wreck and all I cared about was making sure Adrian was okay. He had a bloody lip, as I remembered. And he was angry from the phone call.

But what was in that safe?

All at once, my memories flashed back and my eyes darted to the big mahogany desk in the middle of the room. The tattered red book still lay in the same spot that Adrian had placed it. Out of an entire library full of books, why was this one locked away, hidden from everything else?

Was Samael's Father referring to this book? And if he was, that would be admitting he was more than just a dream. It would be admitting to myself that all of them were real.

I felt myself gravitating toward the desk and gripped Adrian's dusty red book. Turning it over in my hands, I gave it a closer examination. The title on the spine read, *"The Children's Book of Jewish Folklore."*

Why would Adrian, a person with a complete lack of faith, keep such a book locked away? Immediately, I began to scan the pages searching for any sort of clue.

I flipped through the musty yellow pages as I admired the illustrations. The drawings all looked similar to what you would find in just about any bible but there was one specific drawing that caught my attention. It was an ominous illustration of the Garden of Eden.

There were dead apple trees and withered branches reaching up toward a black sky. There were overgrown weeds dancing up the steel gates which were closed and chained. It was not like any picture of Eden I'd ever seen before. This was the Garden after the gates had locked. Growing more curious by the second, I turned the page and began scanning the words. The story looked similar to the one I had known, but there were additional characters I had never heard of before. Then my body froze in horror as my eyes focused on one word only.

How is this possible?

Printed in the black ink, I read *his* name.

I couldn't believe my eyes, and I even tried to blink it away but the name remained in the book, dancing over all of the pages as though it were taunting me. The room began to close in on me and the phantom pain in my head returned. I reached for my purse and frantically ingested two more pills, hoping to get a grip on my mental breakdown. Pinching myself as hard as I could, I determined this time I was not dreaming. I sat down on the hard floor and went back to the beginning of the bible. This was one story I needed to read.

According to Adrian's book, God had started off with Adam, creating him from dirt, but he had also made a wife for Adam, also out of dirt. Her name was Lilith.

Since Adam and Lilith were made from equal parts, Lilith refused to submit to Adam, which created an issue. Lilith eventually left and then God created Eve from Adam's rib bone, obviously learning from His first miscalculation.

Now that this female was made *from* Adam, she would have no choice but to submit to her superior man.

As I read this, I realized that among His other faults, God was also a sexist. Eve submitted as she was supposed to until she met Samael, who was Lilith's brother. Christians have always believed him to be Lucifer.

The Devil wears many faces.

Oh my God, no.

I forced the memory of the dream out of my mind and continued reading. The next line caught my full attention as I read it over and over again.

He is a figure who is accuser, seducer, and destroyer, and has been regarded as both good and evil.

Suddenly I couldn't help but compare the green eyes Samael had possessed to Adrian's eyes. Was it pure coincidence that Adrian came into my life right after my dreams began?

That these dreams accelerated once I let him into my life and now, was it just a huge coincidence that Adrian had the very book that held the answers to my questions? My mind raced towards denial.

No way. I refuse to believe what that old man said. Adrian is not Samael.

I pushed the speculations out of my mind and kept reading. Using my finger as a guide, I read each word as if my life depended on it. Eve and Samael fell in love and began an affair better known as *"eating the forbidden fruit."* It was Eve and Samael's adultery that resulted in her and Adam being kicked out of the Garden.

It wasn't an apple—it was illicit sex?

I closed the big red book and rubbed my eyes, glancing over at the clock. It was 10:14 a.m. and I knew Adrian would be waking soon.

What was I going to tell him?

That he was right last night? Maybe my mind *had* summoned him along with some old man who just might be God, and came to me in a dream last night telling me my new lover was the Devil?

The story in Adrian's book was making my head spin. How could I have dreamt some folklore I had never known about? Why did Adrian have this book? What was the connection?

Accuser, Seducer, and Destroyer.

As I analyzed it, Adrian fit the bill here, accusing Ray of being unworthy of my love, seducing me . . . but what had he destroyed? When he came into my life, my relationship was *already* self-destructing. If anything, he'd helped awaken me to my reality.

I flipped to the beginning of the book and decided to read the first chapter. After the first few lines, I decided I didn't care for this book and concluded it held the same hypocritical views as any other religious book I'd ever picked up.

Like my previous encounters with religion, the book made me question the way I was living, and for that, I hated it. The entire first chapter was dedicated to the explanation of evil, stating that evil could be as simple as pernicious selfishness and a drive for immediate gratification without regard for others.

Here I was blaming Ray all this time for chasing after his silly little rock and roll dream but maybe I was the one being selfish for wishing he would give it up and come home to me. My drive for immediate gratification would explain why I continue to gravitate towards Adrian. With Ray's absence, I felt the need to fill the empty void inside of me with the presence of another man. I had carelessly ignored the fact that Ray disliked it because I was being selfish. Or as this book said, I was being evil.

This was B.S. to me.

I slammed the red cover shut and choked on the giant dust cloud that whooshed out.

This was exactly why I despised religion. It would literally make you crazy if you allowed it to get inside your head.

I wasn't evil for having these feelings inside of me. There were much simpler words to describe what was inside of me and evil was not one of them. Lonely, perhaps, sad even, but not evil. I was simply human and the feelings I felt for Adrian were real, hence I would not allow this manipulative little book to shame me for my genuine feelings.

Speaking of which, what were my feelings for Adrian? A minute ago I was planning my escape route out of his life and now . . .

I sat in the middle of the library and rocked back and forth as I hugged my knees. Unable to contain my curiosity, I found myself being pulled back to the dusty red book. Reluctantly opening the pages, I laid my eyes on the next chapter. The text read, *"God created all things living, and then He created man. God named the man Adam, and the woman He named Lilith."*

There was that name again.

Who was she?

Samael's father told me that Adrian had a sister, and they were both evil. Could Lilith be that woman in the Garden? My mind was scaring me, and I needed to get off this mental roller coaster ASAP or my brain would snap. What I was reading sounded way too similar to my dreams.

Not knowing what else to do, I grabbed my phone and punched in the numbers I had dialed so many times in the past. There was only one person who could help me understand all this.

Ray answered on the first ring.

I was actually surprised my call even went through. Despite my abrupt withdrawal from him last night, he had still unblocked my number and accepted my call.

He sounded tired. "What do you want, Sid?" He was obviously drained, almost like he no longer had the energy to keep entertaining the thought of us being happy together.

"Ray!" I shouted into the receiver. I didn't have time to worry about the state of our relationship at that moment, I needed help. "Think about all the books you've ever read . . . did Adam and Eve ever take up other lovers?"

He postponed my question. "Sid, I'm about to go to church and explain to my parents why you're not with me. Can we discuss philosophy later?"

"No, it's important!" I shouted, tears spilling down my cheeks as confusion washed over me. I felt like I was drowning in a sea of bewildering turbulence, the angry waves slamming me into the jagged rocks.

I needed to get my footing back onto solid ground. I needed the water out of my lungs and air to clear my foggy brain.

"No, Sid. I've never read a religion that spoke of Adam and Eve mating with other partners. God created them to be mated to each other for life."

"What about Lilith? You never read about her?"

There was a long pause.

"Is this some kind of trap to try to get me in trouble? I told you already. I'm not seeing Lilly anymore."

I hung up on him. Ray couldn't help me, and I really didn't feel like discussing his manipulative little mistress. I eagerly crawled back to the book and frantically began searching the chapter where I had left off.

I found the yellowed page and skimmed through, reading the words faster than my brain could process. I felt as if I were trying to decipher the da Vinci code. The story continued, stating that Adam and Lilith were created from the same dirt of the earth and that there was no master or leader but instead, a whole lot of bickering.

Lilith told Adam, "*I will not be below you, in life or during sex. I want the superior position.*"

Oh my.

I don't know if it was Ray's earlier comparison but now my mind went directly to Lilly. It sounded like something that slut would say.

Going on with my unorthodox bible lesson, the story explained that Adam argued with Lilith that *he* was the superior one. He eventually sought God's counsel and being the sexist that He was, God agreed with Adam.

Lilly became so enraged that she changed form and flew into the air, disappearing out of sight. God sent three angels to overtake Lilith and return her to Adam, but she refused. And as her rebellion increased, she changed again, becoming more and more ugly and demonic.

As a result, she became a succubus.

I sat back and took a short break from the good book. I could not get Lilith out of my mind. I grabbed my phone and Googled the word, "*succubus.*" It was defined as a demonic woman who appears in dreams and takes the form of a human being, seducing men with her beauty.

What if my dreams really were true? Would that mean Lilly is Lilith?

I read the definition over and over again. It seemed to explain everything. If this was true, then no wonder Ray cheated on me with Lilly. He never stood a chance.

Then my mind drifted over to Adrian and I wondered if men could be a succubus, too. He fit the definition as well.

No. He's not evil. I'll never believe it.

I returned to my reading. The story went on to describe that during the time of Adam and Eve, there was a great war in heaven between God and Lucifer, who had assembled one-third of all Angels to fight against their Heavenly Father for supremacy. God prevailed over Lucifer and his angels and cast them onto earth. Lucifer continued to fight even though he was eternally doomed. God allowed Lucifer to roam the earth until his final defeat at the end of the world. There was no mention of hell in this bible. Instead, it stated that God had thrown Lucifer to *earth*.

Adrian's words were being brought to the forefront of my memory now. He had told me over and over that hell was *earth*. And now I was reading those exact words in this mysterious book.

How did Adrian know?

The doors to the library flung open and I jumped up, startled by the intrusion. Adrian stood in the doorway rubbing the sleep from his eyes. "You had me worried for a minute. I thought maybe you'd left."

I gripped the red book and waved it dramatically as if I'd just discovered some sort of incriminating evidence against him. "Why do you have this book?"

He glanced around the room and flashed me that famous half-smile of his as he took a step towards me. "We are standing in the middle of a library, Sidney. There are thousands of books in here."

I stepped back, keeping the distance between us.

Adrian noticed this and raised his eyebrows.

I challenged him again. "I watched you take this book out of that safe. This book is special to you, Adrian. I want to know why."

For the first time since I'd known him, Adrian's mask of serenity slightly faded as he tried to take another step towards me and watched as I again retreated. "Why are you so worried about that book, Sidney?"

Again, he moved closer, so I danced around the desk, keeping the stationary object between us.

"What's your real name?" I demanded.

"What do you remember?" he asked, his voice eager as he continued to chase after me.

I shouted, "I know who you are. You're Samael."

He froze.

Finally giving up the chase, or silently calculating his next move, we stood in the library, facing off.

And then the doorbell rang.

Adrian put his finger in the air while his eyes lingered on my face. "Don't move," he instructed as he spun around and headed towards the front door.

For some unknown reason, I decided to follow him. I did so possibly to defy his order or to simply run out of the house once the door opened. But when the door did open, I stood there in utter shock with my mouth gaping in horror.

The instant Adrian greeted the visitor my heart plummeted into my stomach. I couldn't believe who I was seeing. She stood on the porch, tall and beautiful in her sheer floral print kimono top and white undershirt. Her long, milky legs were sensually revealing in her tiny denim cutoff shorts. She removed her big sunglasses, unleashing those distinctive catlike green eyes as her red lips curled up in a satisfied smile as she gleefully watched me unravel from the inside out.

What the hell was she doing here?

She ran her long pale hand through her deep red hair as she smiled at my lover.

"Lil," Adrian growled.

I gasped inwardly. *They know each other?*

"Oh my God." I threw my hands up to cover my mouth, but the words had already escaped. Adrian's head shot in my direction. He gave me a look of grave concern as he detected the trembling in my voice.

"Sidney, this is . . ." He began the introduction before the bitch so rudely cut him off.

"Sidney Sinclair," she said, waving her hand, dismissing Adrian's attempt at civility. "We've met. Turns out we have a lot in common, a certain man in particular."

She flashed me her vicious smile and winked.

This cannot be happening, I thought as the walls of the old house began to close in on me.

"I have to go," I exclaimed.

"Where are your manners?" Lilly asked Adrian, completely ignoring my outburst. "Aren't you going to invite me in?"

"Come in, Lil," Adrian responded like a puppet.

She stepped over the threshold and onto the wooden floor. Her black stilettos crushed the ground below her, making a hollow sound ring in my ears. Adrian scurried to the porch, collecting her bags as if he was now the butler and the woman of the house had just arrived home. I had never seen him so compliant in my life. It disgusted me and I couldn't bear to watch anymore. I had seen enough. I pushed past Adrian and hustled down the steps of the porch, passing the ancient flagpole.

"Sidney!" Adrian yelled.

I didn't turn around, instead I just ran faster.

I had always known Adrian had someone in his past so it should have come as no surprise to finally meet her. What I wasn't prepared for was that it was the same woman who had ruined my life by using her black magic on my beloved Ray.

As if that wasn't bad enough, Adrian was now just as spellbound as Ray.

The Father was right. She was *evil*.

* * *

Taking my heels off and clutching them in my arms, I padded up the wooden steps of Granny's Craftsman home and burst through the front door. Chrissy was lying on the couch watching television. She sat up as soon as I entered and sounded like an angry parent as she demanded to know where I had been all night.

"I can't talk about it right now," I mumbled as I shuffled through my purse in search of my pills. I did need to speak to someone who could help me understand why my life seemed to be falling apart but as much as I loved my best friend, I knew she couldn't help me.

In moments like this, Chrissy could be as dense as the forest.

I barely looked at her. Instead, I raced into the bathroom and swallowed several pills before heading straight into Granny's room.

Entering, I gripped the door frame to steady my balance. Once again it felt as if a giant vortex were opening up before my feet and threatening to swallow me whole. My brain was all over the place as if I were walking a tightrope which was threatening to break and send me spiraling down into a black hole. I shuffled over to the old Stickley chair I had sat in so many times before and stared at my sleeping grandmother. She seemed to be the only person left on this earth who still grounded me.

After a few moments of collecting my thoughts, I spoke to her. "Granny, if there was ever a time that I needed you, it's now."

I longingly gazed at the frail woman as I waited for her to respond, but no words came out of her mouth, just shallow breaths. I refused to give up and stared at her, willing her to wake up. I scooted my chair closer to her bed and took her soft hand in mine. Strangely, it was warmer than usual, as if all of a sudden her circulation began working as it did when she was still a young woman, not a frail old shell. Resting my forehead on her hand, I whispered to her, "Should I stay and fight for Adrian?"

Again, I waited for an answer.

No response.

And so, it seemed that with her *silence* she had given me the answer that I needed. The answer I knew to be true all along.

Go back to Ray and be happy.

I decided at that moment I would do just that.

I leaned over and softly kissed her cheek, just in time for something inexplicable to happen. Granny squeezed my hand and inhaled deeply. I was so startled that I jumped back, sending the Stickley chair to the floor. I collected myself and our eyes met.

For the past several months, my ailing Granny's eyes had been normally aged and covered with thick cataracts, causing them to appear dull with a cloudy, blackish blue color. Those same eyes were now open as they stared intently at me. Clear as crystals. No fog impairing them today. She didn't speak to me, she just continued to stare.

"Granny?" I asked. I silently hoped that Doctor Kyle had been wrong all along and that my beloved relative could hear me. I reasoned that all the reading I had been doing with her had brought her back to me. I let out a cry of joy as I wrapped my arms around her neck and sobbed into her chest, but my moment of happiness was short lived when suddenly, Granny's hand reached up and twisted my necklace, squeezing it so tightly it felt like a superhuman skeleton was attacking me. I couldn't breathe as I felt a powerful pull on my *neck*.

The pendant!

I tried to pull away from her grip but my airway had become constricted. I fought back but I could feel the chain searing into my flesh and I began choking.

I couldn't breathe.

The necklace chain was digging deep into my skin and the pendant was in Granny's hand. She kept the pressure on as I continued to struggle for air.

"Let go," I begged through gasps of breath. "Please!"

I could see black dots now clouding my vision as the world around me grew darker. I looked down at Granny's eyes, which were now wide open and filled with a manic intensity. She seethed emotionally, "He's gotten to you, just like he got to your mother." She growled as her hand continued to tighten around the necklace.

With my last ounce of strength, I yanked myself away from her and collapsed onto the wooden floor, clutching my neck and desperately sucking in air. I coughed and tried to regain my composure.

I glanced up to see Chrissy hovering over Granny's bed. Looking at me curiously, she chastised, "What in the hell did you do to her?"

Granny was now trying to sit up in bed and screamed at me to take off the necklace. "It's evil. Evil! He will come for you. You have to destroy the necklace!"

Chrissy struggled with my grandmother as I sat on the floor, watching my granny battling my best friend. I was completely useless. Chrissy grabbed a needle from a nightstand drawer and whispered to me apologetically, "I'm going to have to sedate her."

As I watched the sedative slowly take its toll on my relative, I remembered Granny's words of warning.

Just like he got to your mother.

What did she mean?

Why was everybody speaking in riddles?

My mind cleared for a moment and I remembered my mother's journals I had discovered the day Chrissy and I had cleaned out Granny's closet. I scurried out of the white room and retreated to my bedroom in search of any clue my mother's journals held.

I rushed to my dresser and snatched the journal from the drawer. Tossing it on the bed, I ran to my closet and pulled out my running shoes and backpack. I decided there was no way I could stay inside of this house at that moment. Not with a crazy grandmother and Chrissy's prying eyes. I grabbed a fresh change of clothes, stripped off my fancy dress, and put on my sweats.

"Where the hell are you going, Sidney? What is your deal?" Chrissy wailed.

She had followed me up to my room and apparently wasn't about to let me leave without some kind of explanation. Slipping my shoes on, I verbally jolted her. I told her what my grandmother had said before she entered the bedroom.

"Granny tried to rip off my necklace and told me that whoever had gotten to my mom was now getting to me." I nodded at the old journal sitting on my bed. "I have to go through my mom's diary and see what Granny was talking about."

Chrissy's eyes got wide. "Holy shit!"

I reacted back, "Well, I wouldn't call this crap holy by any means."

Holy or not, shit was definitely hitting the fan.

I grabbed my cell phone and the orange bottle of pills and tossed them into my pack. As I slung it over my shoulder and headed for the door, Chrissy placed her body in my path.

"So why don't you just take the necklace off and whatever crazy thing you think is happening to you will stop," she said, as she stood there with her chin raised, arms folded as if she was Einstein's clone with her ingenious solution.

I looked at her like she was an idiot.

Whatever crazy things that may have been summoned by some cursed piece of jewelry were not going to simply go away because I removed the chain from around my neck. Chrissy had watched enough horror movies to know that once you've opened Pandora's Box, you can't just close the lid and expect everything to go back to normal.

I closed my eyes and sought the words to deal with Chrissy's ignorance. "It's not that easy, Chrissy. I just need some time on my own to study the journal and figure this out."

"No, Sidney, what you need is sleep. Look at yourself. No one knows where you've been all night and now you're running around like a crazy person. Are you on drugs?"

I rolled my eyes and pushed my way past her. Now she really was sounding like an overbearing parent.

"If Ray calls, can you tell him I'll call him when I get back?" I shouted over my shoulder as I galloped down the stairs.

"Oh, I'll tell Ray, all right. Tell him you went off the deep end!"

My instructions to her were moot. As soon as I opened the door, I slammed into Ray, who was standing on my porch about to knock on the door.

I moaned inwardly, *"Oh no, not Ray . . . not now."*

His backpack was strapped to his shoulders, which told me he had planned on staying for a while. I was instantly hit with so many emotions; happy to see the love of my life standing in front of me, yet annoyed with his timing and completely freaked out about my grandmother's actions.

I don't have the strength to deal with all this right now.

At that moment, my mother was all I cared about. I needed to decode what Granny was trying to say to me. As Ray stood there waiting for me to respond, I was frantically searching through my backpack looking for the journal. With Chrissy's intrusion, I had completely forgotten to grab it.

Shit!

I angrily tossed my backpack onto the floor and took a step back towards the house. "Ray, not a good time."

He ignored my statement and stepped in front of me, preventing me from retreating further into the house. He tossed his backpack down next to mine. His blue eyes were filled with concern as he looked me over. "You look like crap, Sid."

He took a deep breath and I could still hear the tiredness in his voice, "We need to talk."

My mind had a completely different agenda. *I need that damn journal.*

I squeezed past him and raced up the stairs. Ray ran after me shouting, "Sid, wait!"

As I stepped inside my bedroom and quickly scanned the bed, my heart sank into an abyss of shock and confusion. The journal was no longer there.

I was dumbfounded. *What in the hell was going on?*

Chapter Five

King of Hearts

It only took me a few seconds to realize where the journal must have gone. It's not like it grew legs and walked away. Clenching my fists, I pushed past my needy boyfriend and stomped across the hall and banged on the spare room door, demanding that my best friend come out and face me.

"Unlock this door right now, Chrissy!"

I don't know what Nancy Drew thought she was doing, but it was not going over well with me. I was almost tempted just to kick her out of my house and send her packing back to her father; friendless and unemployed. That would teach her to keep her nose out of other people's business. As I banged on the door, I yelled again for her to let me in.

"No," she shouted. "I'll give you back the journal once you get some sleep, Sidney, but not a second before that."

Looking over at Ray, I pointed at the door with extreme urgency. "Well, don't just stand there. Break the damn thing down!" I ordered.

Ray shifted out of his needy mode and became my champion. He briskly strode across the hallway, and I graciously moved out of the way with a big smile on my face, expecting my man to display his sheer strength and do as I instructed. But instead of slamming his shoulder against the door, he snatched me by my arm and yanked me back into my bedroom.

"Ray, what are you doing? I need you to bust down that door."

I struggled with him, but I was no match against his strong arms. Ray slammed my bedroom door shut and looked at me as if I had three heads. He gripped my shoulders and held me in place and yelled at me to stop fighting. Finally, I stopped struggling and looked at him. Worry was written all over his face.

He was gravely concerned. "What in the hell is going on with you, Sid?" he whispered, out of breath.

All it took was that one look from him to make me realize that maybe I was overreacting a bit. Maybe Chrissy and Ray were not the ones out of step here. Maybe I was the odd woman out.

I reasoned to myself that I could take a few winks of sleep and then Chrissy would calmly hand me the journal. Slowly, I began to catch my breath as I fell into a calmer sense of serenity.

Now, as I stood looking at Ray, I realized this was the first time I had seen him since he had proposed to me and since I'd made the mistake with Adrian.

All I wanted to do was rush into his arms and erase the last twenty-four hours from my memory. He was everything I had ever wanted and just when I finally had him back in my life, I had gone and screwed it up.

Way to go, Sidney.

I leaned against the wall and looked at his tired face, waiting for him to tear into me about last night's desertion. Instead, he tilted his head and began speaking, much softer than I could have imagined.

First, he asked if I was all right.

After I nodded my head, he quickly explained why he was there in the first place. "I think I may have rushed into things last night. I never meant to scare you off or make you run away. If you want to wait to marry me, that's fine. I just want to be with you."

His sweetness was killing me. Couldn't he just be the asshole I'd gotten used to dealing with? With each word that came out of his mouth, I felt like a bigger piece of trash. I was riddled with guilt and my conscience was eating me alive. I couldn't take his kindness when I knew I didn't deserve it.

"I slept with him," I blurted out.

I wanted to come clean about my actions.

I closed my eyes and waited for the chaos to erupt but it was sheer silence. The ongoing silence grew into an unbearable torture until I could no longer take it. I opened my eyes and looked at Ray.

His reaction was far worse than I could have anticipated.

I watched as Ray's happy face slowly transformed into a mass of raw emotions. I suddenly wished I could take my statement back. We stood staring at each other for what seemed like an eternity. Ray's lips were contorted, he was desperately trying to speak, but words failed him. He took a step back in a pitiful attempt to regain his composure. He opened his mouth to try again, but still the words remained paralyzed on his tongue. Nothing.

He was the Sphinx.

As I buried the knife deeper into his heart, I needlessly added the *object* of my lustful tryst, "With Adrian," I confirmed. "I slept with Adrian."

If Ray was silent before, he was downright comatose now. He stood there silently, unable to speak. His icy blue eyes stabbed into my guilty soul. The expression on his face revealed his pain.

I had devastated him.

He finally brought both hands up to his face and rubbed his eyes excessively in a futile attempt to obliterate the image of me lying in Adrian's arms. In that exact moment I lost any comprehension of how I really felt.

Obviously I regretted what I had done, and I felt extremely sorry, but on the other hand, I felt a righteous sense of payback. I was finally able to return all of the pain he'd heaped upon me over the past year with that whore back in L.A. I finally found an emotional chink in his armor and it felt exhilarating.

Maybe I really was evil.

Or just *female*.

Ray quickly rebounded. He had allowed himself to come apart for just five minutes. Then his massive ego kicked in and he was back in control of his emotions. That was to be expected from someone as self-centered and self-absorbed as he.

He removed his hands from his eyes and shot me a withering glance that quickly dissipated my temporary feelings of triumph. It was a look of pure disgust.

"Dammit, Sid," he shouted as he punched the plaster on the wall inches from the right side of my face. I fell to the floor, placing my hands over my head to protect myself as the memories from that night in front of the bar came rushing back to me.

As soon as he saw me cowering on the floor, he abruptly stopped his crazy behavior and did the strangest thing I have ever seen him do. *He* began to apologize to *me*.

Profusely.

I didn't know what kind of parallel universe we had entered where Ray apologized to *me* for cheating on him, but I stood up and took responsibility. "Ray, I'm so sorry."

And I was truly sorry. I now fully regretted that moment of weakness. I should have stayed and fought for Ray. I loved him so much and now it hurt me to see him upset.

The things he had done to me were different. They were under different circumstances. Ray had genuinely felt affection for Lilly. I hated her but he had real emotions for her. What I had done was spiteful and wrong. I had *used* Adrian to punish Ray for hurting me. I could see that

I had made a terrible mistake. I reached up and cradled Ray's head in my arms and began to weep. "I screwed up, Ray. Please forgive me."

He said nothing but I could feel the vibration of his shaking body. He was sobbing too. We sat together against the broken wall, holding each other and feeling miserable until I gave in to my much needed sleep.

* * *

I awoke to the harmonious sound of the piano that only one member in my household knew how to play. The afternoon sun shone through the window, but the fall air still made the house cold. I discovered my tan fur blanket draped across me. Ray must have laid it on me as I slept.

He still cares enough to not let me freeze to death.

I arose and groggily followed the sound of the music. I had to face it eventually. Entering the living room, I stood with the blanket around me as I listened to him play. He never looked up but he must have known I was watching him because when the song ended, he patted the bench, signaling for me to sit down next to him.

I joined him and allowed the blanket to fall down from my shoulders, preferring Ray's body warmth to comfort me. I scooted closer to him, but stopped when I felt the tension in his body grow. It seemed he was having enough trouble with me just sitting next to him. Touching him may have been his breaking point. I sat silently, giving him space as he reassembled his feelings. Ray reached out to put the blanket back on me, but stopped inches from my skin. His hand sat there hovering in mid-air.

"I can't touch you." He gritted through his teeth. His voice had an angry edge to it.

I just stared in disbelief. After everything we had been through, he wasn't going to forgive me for this. His look of disgust and fury was back. It was that same look I had seen earlier.

My heart sank. This was not over by a long shot.

Ray began to verbally tear me apart. "You're not pure anymore, Sid. He's contaminated you."

I fought back. "How many people have *you* contaminated, Ray?"

"It's not the same, Sid! You were mine, only mine. It doesn't matter who I'd been with because I was going to marry you! Now I can't even look at you. Every time I touch you from now on, I'll be thinking about you touching him. Every time I kiss you, I'll be wondering if you were wishing it was his lips on yours. I can't live like that."

"Live like what, Ray . . . like me? Because that was me you just described. My life for the past year has been hell thanks to you and your whore."

All of my feelings of self-doubt had been implanted in my brain by him and his infidelity for months. I angrily stared at him, refusing to allow him to give up on us that easily. After moments of silence, I began wondering if my words were sinking into that thick skull of his.

"I made a mistake," I admitted as I continued to plead my case. "But I'm still the same person I've always been, Ray. I still love you."

He shook his head and looked away without saying another word. Sitting next to Ray on the piano bench, I'd never felt so alone in my life. I always thought the worst pain I had ever experienced was my own heartbreak, but today I realized that was not the case. Watching Ray's heart break at my hands proved to be much more painful.

I sat in silence with no words of solace to offer him.

Finally, Ray closed the lid to the piano keys and rested his elbows on top of the wood, lost in thought. He took a deep breath, as if preparing for a long speech and turned to look at me.

Exhaling, he asked me, "Did you buy my CD?"

Now, I was appalled. At a moment when our relationship was on the brink of disaster, he had asked me if I had bought his *album?*

He was just as narcissistic as Chrissy.

Before I had time to answer, he got up and strode across the room to where his backpack was resting. Fumbling through the contents, he pulled out a CD and returned to his spot on the piano bench, handing me the case.

"What are you going to do, sign it for me?" I asked him, unable to mask the bitterness in my voice.

"Just read the testimonials section."

I opened up the jewel case and searched for the page where each band member gets a small paragraph to write their thanks. I searched for Ray's paragraph and it was filled with multiple names from the industry. The first name was just as foreign as the last, confirming my fears that I didn't know Ray at all anymore. Our circles were completely different now.

Then I caught a glimpse of one familiar name which automatically made me cringe.

Rene. I rolled my eyes and moved on to the next line, before seeing something that was more than just meaningless names of music moguls, a sentence at the end. It was a simple sentence that the average reader may not comprehend. There was only one person who could decipher its meaning, and she was reading it right now.

My bottom lip began to involuntarily tremble as my brain put together its message.

Head Club is playing over and over on repeat. No matter what I do, I can't get it to stop.

Ray was telling me that the quality that annoyed him most about me was inadvertently happening to him. He never could stand the fact that I related every song, movie, and book to my life and now he was admitting that a song was stuck in his mind, defining *his* life.

And that song told me everything I'd wanted to hear. "Head Club" was one of my favorite songs. It was a simple song with only one verse before the singer began to bellow his heartbreak into the microphone, saying how sick he was of writing all his songs about one singular person.

The song related to us and what had happened that night at the bar so much that Ray himself could have written the lyrics. I looked up at him and met those baby blues.

Why would he add this message into his song booklet?

I thought he wanted nothing more to do with me when he left. He had blocked my phone calls and had excluded me from his social media. He had put up a barrier and shut me out from his world, never once looking back.

So why would this specific song still be playing in his head?

"I was half expecting you to call my name out your window, you know?" he said tenderly.

Another lyric from the song.

I knew he was referring to the morning he must have posted bail and came back to get his car from my driveway.

"I overslept," was all I could manage to say.

And it was true.

I would have screamed his name from the top of my lungs that morning from my window if I had gotten the chance. I would have attached myself to his body like an amoeba and never let go, begging him to stay, and if he somehow had gotten himself free, I would have jumped on the hood of his car so he couldn't have driven out of my life. I would have done anything to keep him there. But it was true, I had overslept. When I awakened he was gone and my hell had begun in earnest.

"The night I went to jail. I called Rene and asked her to post my bail and she refused to do it."

I opened my mouth to remind him what a heartless bitch she was, but Ray put his hand up, asking me not to interrupt him.

"Rene refused to post my bail as long as I continued to see you. She was livid about the huge mess the PR team was going to have to clean up, not to mention the team of lawyers that had to be hired to keep that clueless detective off my case."

Even though the lid to the piano was closed, Ray's fingers still tapped on the wood as if playing some silent tune in his head. He was processing everything. That was Ray.

He turned his head to me and I saw that those blue ocean pools were filled with tears. "They made me do what I fought so hard not to. They made me choose the music over you. Rene tried to sugar coat it by telling me it was only temporary. That once the tour was over I could contact you again. But if I tried so much as to sneak a message from my family to you, they would fire me. Communication with you would be a breach of my contract and they could legally remove me from the band."

I was shocked.

All this time, I thought that Ray had deserted me *intentionally*. Now I was hearing our separation had been forced. These past six months had been just as hard on him as it had been for me. I didn't know what else to do but to reach into my pocket and pull out my handy orange bottle.

Ray gripped my fingers before I could twist off the top.

"No," he said forcefully. I raised my eyebrow in question, but he stood his ground. "You don't need these pills, Sid. Your injuries healed months ago. There's no reason you should still be taking these."

Chrissy had been telling me the same thing for months but I always argued with her. I maintained the fact that my body still hurt, that I was filled entirely with the worst degree of pain imaginable, usually forcing Chrissy to relent. But as Ray said this to me, I suddenly realized he was right. The pain I had been attempting to conceal over the past six months was the pain of losing him. I no longer had to worry about that.

Ray was here with me now—this time for good.

Then he took that familiar black box out of his pocket and rested it on top of the piano. As I stared at it, he continued. "I bought this for you the morning I got out of jail. Sure, I was still pissed at you. But I knew you were the one I wanted to be with forever."

Ray paused, staring at me.

He was waiting for a response, but I couldn't speak. All I could do was gaze helplessly at that black velvet box.

He followed my eyes. "That little box was the only thing that got me through each day. That ring and the calendar. I counted down each day waiting for the tour to end so I could take that box, get down on one knee, and ask you to marry me. I never figured I might be too late."

The last line shook me out of my stupor.

"Too late?" I questioned.

Finally feeling the severity of my mistake, I realized Ray may no longer *want* to marry me. The tables had turned. All night, I was so unsure about accepting his proposal but now it seemed I was being rebuffed here.

There was nothing more in the world I wanted than that ring on my finger.

Ray snatched the box and it disappeared into his hand as he straddled the piano bench so his entire body was facing me. He placed it on the bench behind him and took my hands in his.

He asked nervously, "Am I too late?"

I shook my head no.

Ray could never be too late.

Time stood still when he was with me.

He reached behind him, and the box reappeared. He opened it and revealed its sparkling diamond. His words matched the romantic intensity of its sparkling presence.

"I don't care about anything that happened in either of our lives *before* this moment. Let's only look forward. Marry me, Sidney, and we can leave this all behind. We can take Granny and move. We'll go up to my parents' cabin and live in the sticks where nobody cares about fortune and fame. We'll just be Mr. and Mrs. Ryker."

I laughed as the tears of happiness slid down my cheeks. "Okay, Ray, I'll marry you."

He slipped the beautiful ring on my finger, and it fit so perfectly, as if this ring had always been meant for me.

I knew in my heart it was true.

This time, we would be happy forever.

Chapter Six

Turn it Off

I still had to go to work, but Ray couldn't wait to begin our new lives as Mr. and Mrs. Ryker. We agreed I would finally give Bob my two-week notice.

Ray was going to the hospital to get all of the paperwork done in order to have Granny transported to the cabin and away from the haunting memories our little town continuously seemed to inflict on all of us.

I thought with more than a little elation, *I'm finally leaving this place once and for all.*

I kissed Ray goodbye as we stood in the doorframe of Granny's home.

"Have a nice day, soon-to-be Mrs. Ryker. See you at dinner," he said softly as he refused to loosen his grip on me.

I smiled at my new name, clutching onto him just as tightly. "Be sure to keep your lips sealed until I get home. I want to be with you when we tell your parents."

Ray nodded with a smile plastered across his face. "Remember to give Bob your notice. Two weeks and then we're gone. We're never coming back here, Sid."

I never thought those words could make me so happy. I was finally going to escape this place of torment. Sneaking one more kiss, I reluctantly let go of my handsome fiancé and headed towards the truck.

Four more hours and then I'll get to see him again, I thought with a perma-grin melded on my face.

Work was a breeze as I skipped around the store, happy to show off my ring to anyone who seemed the slightest bit interested. The magnificent piece of jewelry overwhelmed my finger and seemed to generate conversation all on its own.

I thought telling Bob I was quitting was going to be difficult, but it actually proved to be just the opposite.

It felt liberating.

I think we both knew this was a long time coming. He even offered to put in a transfer request to a different store further north but I politely declined the offer. I knew Ray and I would have limited time to ourselves before he would have to go back out on the road, and I wanted to ensure that every second leading up to that point would be spent with my future husband.

Of course, thoughts of Adrian still danced around my brain. At first the tiny movements were like a subtle ballerina, barely scratching the surface with her tiny delicate feet. But as the day progressed, the thoughts grew stronger until they were like an intense tap dancer pounding forcefully on my brain. Despite my orders, my mind refused to forget him.

I did my best to ignore them. I had moved on.

But my dreams continued to replay in my brain. They continued to haunt me with their vividness. There had to be some logical explanation for it all, beginning with the Garden. Perhaps Granny did read that distorted bible story to me as a child and somehow in the back of my subconscious, it seemed to resurface when I slept. But that still didn't explain why Adrian had that book. He also didn't deny it when I accused him of being Samael. That was not part of my dream. That was real.

I shook the thoughts out of my head and continued with my tasks at work. It no longer mattered who Adrian was or how he had become associated with Lilly. I was leaving this town behind and in it, I was leaving Adrian. Ray had forgiven me for my mistake and now it was time to focus on him and us.

Adrian had Lilly now and they could both try to swallow the bullshit they fed to each other. They could both choke on it for all I cared. Lilly was a masochistic bitch and if that's the kind of company he kept, then I wanted nothing more to do with him. I couldn't believe that all this time I had felt sorry for Adrian's sad feelings of lost love only to find out it was over *her*. It made me sick with anger. As I prepared to leave the store that evening, I banished the unpleasant thoughts from my brain. I said goodbye to Bob and headed out, eager to spend the night with my fiancé.

* * *

The first thing I noticed when I arrived home from work that evening was the broken glass. Tiny shards of crystal littered the front porch.

Crunch. Crunch. Crunch.

What the hell?

It sounded like I was walking across hard, frozen snow as my shoes crushed the glass below. Following the path of destruction with my eyes, I saw the big picture window had been shattered and the front door was ajar. I could feel my blood turn to ice as I realized what may have happened. I had defied the killers' order to stay away from Ray and . . .

Had they returned?

Immediately, I pushed through the door and sprinted to Granny's bedroom. I collapsed in relief upon seeing my dear relative lying in her bed. She was alive, her chest slowly rising before falling back down into her stomach.

"Oh Granny," I breathed, as I tried to calm myself down and think of a rational explanation for the broken window. Maybe Ray had accidentally locked himself out and he had no choice but to break the window in order to regain entry into the house?

Scratching my head, I slowly climbed to my feet, not convinced. My work was less than a mile down the road. If Ray needed to get into the house, he could have just stopped by the store and asked for the key.

Walking over to inspect my Granny a bit more thoroughly, I noticed something that I hadn't seen the first time around.

As her chest rose up, so did a piece of paper.

Its edge was curled up, flapping like the delicate wing of a sparrow with the motions of Granny's breathing.

It was a note addressed to me.

I took a few steps closer as the warning bells began blaring in my ears. The handwriting was familiar. I had seen it before, when I lay in the hospital bed the day after the attack in my backyard. Detective Albright had given me the note which had the same recognizable penmanship. It had been written by the *same* person who killed Nouri.

I gingerly picked the note up off Granny's chest and began to read it. In the two seconds it took to piece together the words so eloquently scrawled across the paper, my perfect world collapsed.

"Why take old when you can have new? Granny's safe, but Ray may be singing a different tune. I'd rather take him underground than dear old Granny anyway."

Take Ray underground? What could that possibly mean other than to kill him?

I stuffed the note into my back pocket and rushed out of Granny's room in a mad dash to get help.

"Chrissy!" My voice echoed through the silent house.

No answer.

I ran back into the living room, my feet feeling like heavy blocks of sludge.

"Chrissy!" I yelled again.

Standing at the bottom of the stairs, I could see a yellow light protruding from the crack in the bathroom door. She must be taking a shower.

I spun around to retrieve my phone to call Detective Albright. I had to save Ray before it was too late. But as I turned around my eyes met those familiar green eyes that still possessed the ability to take my breath away. Even in the midst of disaster.

Adrian stood in the open entrance of the house. Confusion and worry lined his face. "What happened?" he asked.

"They took Ray," I cried as I rushed towards Adrian, reaching into my back pocket to retrieve the note.

Resilient to my hysterics, Adrian focused only on one thought, "Ray was *here*?"

I shoved the note into Adrian's hand, forcing him to read it. After a long pause, he finally realized he wouldn't get any more details from me until he began to cooperate. Tearing his eyes away from mine, he looked down at the note.

And then his expression changed. It darkened, in the same way it did when he visited me in the hospital after my attack. He focused so hard on the note that I had to nudge him to break his concentration and help me devise a plan.

"What do you think it means?" I asked frantically.

Adrian only stared at the fading scar that graced my hairline as his mouth twisted into a grotesque frown. He held up the note. "Do you think the same person who wrote this note hit you on the head?"

I nodded in response. "Of course they did. Whoever wrote that note murdered Nouri!"

"Lil." He breathed the name so quietly I wasn't even sure I heard him correctly.

I stood still, waiting for Adrian to repeat himself, but he remained frozen, staring at the note. Finally, he looked up at me and I saw a side of him I had never witnessed before.

Adrian was seething. "She's my sister, Sidney. I never told you about her because I haven't seen her in years. She may as well be dead to me."

I was immediately confused. Lilly was Adrian's *sister*?

Isn't that what the man in my dream told me?

I refused to believe it and now the truth was smacking me in the face. I had rationalized to myself that the dreams hadn't been real, that my mind was still groggy with sleep when I accused Adrian of being Samael. But now, the truth was confronting me with cold, hard facts. At that point, I started to silently freak out again, but at the same time, I was a little relieved to hear that Lilly was his sister and not his long lost lover; as I had initially suspected.

"How?" I asked him. It was not a specific question but it was soon to be followed by more detailed ones as they poured out of me. How are my dreams real, how is Lilly your sister? How did she find you? How everything? "I mean, her last name is Lavelle."

Adrian tersely explained the surname. "It's an alias. I had no idea my sister was the one Ray was sleeping with in LA." He put his hands in the air, palms up. "I swear."

I believed him.

"She told me all the gory details after you ran out of the house this morning. I'm really sorry, Sidney. I never meant for you to be hurt by all this."

I shook my head, not ready to get into this. "It doesn't matter right now. All that matters is that I find Ray, right now."

I knew that every time I mentioned Ray's name it was a punch to Adrian's gut, but I had to focus on what was important here. Wherever Ray was, I knew he was running out of time. I had to save him.

"Tell me what you remember," Adrian persisted.

I shot him a look of confusion, laced with impatience.

He clarified his question. "You called me Samael this morning. What do you remember?"

I shook my head, becoming angry with the time we were losing to find Ray. "It was just a dream I've been having. You reminded me of him. That's all. Please help me," I begged.

I could see Adrian struggling with himself, deciding whether he wanted to help or not. After a few more seconds of indecision, he finally let out a sigh of defeat, and reluctantly agreed to help me. "Okay, I think I know where they might be."

Chapter Seven

Burn Bright

It was getting dark as we approached the cemetery that evening. It was late September, and the days were growing shorter. As darkness enveloped the small town of Noddington Heights, I sensed a sort of evil seep into the graveyard.

Adrian was trudging a few steps ahead of me and I had to run to keep up with him. He was not happy about helping me find Ray.

As soon as I saw the brick and wrought iron entrance it seemed the sky grew even darker, with a semblance of fog.

A creepy kind of mist was rolling in.

It reminded me of a time years ago, when Chrissy and I had taken a walk through the cemetery at midnight on Halloween. We had ended up spooking ourselves when we went to exit the gates and noticed a group of raccoons climbing out of the two large oak trees next to the stone pillars. I swear they gave us a threatening look, stood up on their hind legs, and hissed at us. Both Chrissy and I ran away screaming. We found a hole in the cyclone fence and flew underneath it. We even took the long way back to the car to ensure we steered clear of those little beasts.

Tonight, as Adrian and I entered the cemetery, I had a feeling that what waited for us was much worse than a pack of wild raccoons.

Adrian seemed to accelerate his pace as he began to climb the dirt hill leading up to his family's mausoleum.

"Can you please slow down?" I shouted.

He reached into his denim pockets and pulled out his only stress reliever. Stopping at the top of the hill, he thumped the cigarette box against his hand, ripped the cellophane pack open with his teeth, spit the wrapper on the ground, and pulled a cancer stick out of the box.

While waiting for me, he cupped his hands around it and lit his cigarette. He inhaled and slowly released the toxic poisons from his mouth just as I finally caught up to him. They crossed through the air directly towards me, causing me to cough as I felt the damn smoke violate my nose. He was slowly killing me with his bad habits.

Then, he turned serious. "I need to talk to you about last night."

He was not going to let this go.

Exhausted and out of breath, I plopped down on the dirt next to his feet. Staring straight ahead, unable to look at him, I blurted out, "Last night was a mistake."

I didn't look up to see his reaction. I couldn't face him.

After a few agonizing seconds of silence, I heard his feet pound against the earth as he headed towards his family's crypt. I slowly picked myself up off the ground and followed him, intentionally keeping my distance.

As we descended the steps, I realized why Adrian had thought of this place. The note mentioned taking Ray underground and this crypt was hidden beneath the earth. The missive made perfect sense. I just hoped we weren't too late.

When we finally made it to the mausoleum, I was flooded with disappointment. It was empty. "Where could they be?" I cried, panic beginning to set in.

But Adrian no longer chose to humor me, he had some issues of his own he still wanted to resolve. "We lit this fire, Sidney. Nobody else helped us. It was us. Now you're standing in front of me saying it was a *mistake?*"

I stood there with my arms crossed, completely confused. At this point, I didn't know if I was making the right decision or not. Every second spent with Adrian seemed right. But now with Lilly in the picture, and those dreams, things were getting too weird.

Besides, how could I just throw away the last two and a half years with Ray? How could I work so hard at something I wanted so badly and when I finally got it, walk away?

He had proposed to me. I couldn't abandon what Ray and I had now. Furthermore, I couldn't abandon Ray. He was in danger and I had to find him.

"Ray's not here. We should go," I suggested.

"Just answer me truthfully, Sidney. Was it really a mistake?"

We stood on the cold brick floor staring at each other. Adrian was determined, waiting for an answer to his question, but I couldn't say it. The minutes crept by and soon the sun disappeared from the sky. Eventually, we had to light a sconce to see inside the dreary tomb. Even then, I couldn't deliver the answer Adrian wanted from me.

"I love you, Sidney. And you said you loved me too. Do you even understand what that word means because so far in your life, everyone that tells you they love you has left you. Your mom, your dad, and Ray."

His words hurt, even if it was the truth.

"I've stayed in this town for you, Sidney. I would trade everything to stay with you. Can't you see that?"

I carefully tried to soften my words in a way that would hurt Adrian as little as possible. But this wasn't going to be easy.

I quickly learned there was no painless way to tell him, and I watched his face as each one of my words hit him like an emotional fist. "Everything you're saying about me is the exact same way I feel about Ray."

He lifted his hands up to his head and began running them through his long black hair in frustration. Taking one last long drag on his cigarette, he flicked it on the ground and stomped the ember out.

"I warned you, Sidney. I warned you before we even got involved to be sure that you knew what you wanted. I told you I don't play games. I play for keeps. I thought you understood that."

"I thought that was what I wanted too. But that was before . . ."

I stopped talking. I had said too much.

Adrian had no idea about Ray's proposal and at the moment, he didn't seem stable enough to hear it. He was beginning to frighten me and I wasn't sure if he could handle that kind of news right now.

He caught my abrupt stop. He knew I was hiding something. He walked directly over to me, never taking his eyes off of mine. I took a step back but there was nothing but a wall behind me. I had no place to go. Once again I was trapped with him.

"Before what?" he questioned, searching my eyes, looking for any hint of deception. I looked at the ground, but he grabbed my chin with his hand and forced me to hold his gaze. "You thought you wanted me before *what*, Sidney?" he demanded.

I bit my lower lip in anticipation of his anger and revealed only part of the truth; the obvious part. "Before Ray and I got back together, Adrian. I've decided to stay with him."

Releasing me, Adrian took a step back and automatically reached for his pocket. I put my hand on his but he cringed at my touch. Ignoring his dejection, I nodded towards his cigarettes. "Please don't," I begged. "You know how I feel about those."

He blinked, his eyes mixed with disbelief and a little bit of contempt at the nerve I had to ask him to do anything. It broke my heart for him to look at me like that.

He took a couple steps back and defiantly pulled out the cigarette against my wishes.

"What is it about him, Sidney? I've given you everything he refused to give you. Why aren't I enough?"

I really didn't want to have this conversation with him. I wrapped my arms around my chest and answered, "It's complicated, Adrian. The history I have with Ray can't just be forgotten."

Adrian dropped his unlit cigarette and stomped towards me. He gripped my arm as he shouted in my face, "What about *our* history?!" His question echoed off the stone walls, reverberating angrily in my ears.

He let go of my arm and ran his hand through his sweaty hair. Then he reached down and gripped the emerald pendant hanging from my neck. "You told me you'd never forget me," he growled.

His words transported my memory back to those dreams. I knew I had never once uttered those words to Adrian, but Eve had said them to Samael. Things were getting weird again and I didn't have the energy to deal with this. Besides, I still had to find Ray. I pushed past Adrian in an attempt to leave but then he continued his jealous rant.

"I meant what I said, you know."

I looked back at Adrian, feeling a little more than a bit confused. I had no idea what he was rambling about now.

"I said I wouldn't leave until I got what I came for, Sidney. I'm not leaving without you."

I came back here for someone and I'm not leaving without them.

Adrian had just repeated the line he'd used the first night we met. I stopped walking and turned around. "You didn't even know me then. I couldn't have been what you came here for." I shook my head, thinking of an explanation. "You just got sidetracked along the way."

He hit me with a bomb. "Samael and Eve. Have you dreamt of them?"

I froze.

I hadn't shared those dreams with anyone but my computer. Why would he ask that question? I held the truth on my tongue and said nothing. But I felt my heart pounding now.

He continued, "I may be skeptical of the bible stories *you* read, but those two people are factually real. They're us."

I shook my head in denial. He was not going to take me to Crazy Town with him. "That's impossible, Adrian."

He squinted his eyes at me. "I promised you I would find you and I meant it."

My dreams rushed back to me. I remembered a dream when Samael promised he would find Eve after she had been turned away from the Garden. He had given her a pendant that supposedly contained her memories, her soul as well, and as long as she passed it down to her next of kin, her soul would live on in whatever body it may possess. Could that be what was actually happening now?

Is that what Granny had warned me about?

Eve's soul was in my body, waiting to be reunited with Samael, or as I knew him—Adrian.

I gripped my pendant as I felt all the color draining from my face.

Granny had said Samael was evil, as did his own Father.

My mother had also warned me about him.

Samael didn't seem evil in my dreams. He was just a man in love.

I stood facing Adrian as he waited anxiously for me to process everything he was saying. Was it true that he really could be my soul mate? He had been there through it all. He had been the perfect friend and lover . . . but my soul mate?

I shook the thought from my mind.

I've made my choice, I told myself.

He stepped forward and I attempted to back away but he knew me well. He already suspected my plan, so he gripped my arm to prevent me from moving, then he leaned forward to whisper something in my ear.

I closed my eyes and resisted the urge to jump into his arms. I pulled my arms out of his grip and stuffed my hands in my pockets to ensure they would not defy me and grasp onto him.

"Stop it," I begged, my eyes clenched shut.

But Adrian was insistent. "Open your eyes, Sidney."

I felt my hands creeping out of my pockets, wanting to grip him, but I shoved them even deeper back down into my pants.

"Let me go, please," I pleaded.

But my words seemed to make him cling to me even tighter. "Your body is just a vessel driven by your soul," he whispered as he brushed his soft lips against my ear. "Give in to it."

I closed my eyes, willing him to go away. "I have to go. I can't see you anymore."

It was obvious Ray was not in the cemetery. I had to search for him. Staying down here with Adrian would only lead to more mistakes. I attempted to brush past him but he grabbed my arm in an attempt to stop me. In one swift movement I was in his arms, responding to his urgent kiss.

Damn!

I tried to break away, but I remained in his clutches. "You can't deny what's meant to be, Sidney. Just give in."

I did what he said and it was easier than I thought. Adrian was right. I couldn't deny what was in front of my face. We belonged together, and as we held each other, giving in to our desires, my heart warmed to it.

For a moment.

But then I remembered Ray and my eyes flew open. I violently pushed Adrian away. Just in time to see two figures step out of the darkness and appear in the light.

Ray stood there with a strange expression on his tanned face and I knew he had just witnessed me kissing Adrian.

Lilly was behind him, pressing a pearl-handled revolver to his back and wearing a smile to die for.

Chapter Eight

Hang 'Em High

Adrian met Ray's eyes and intentionally licked his lips, as if savoring the kiss that was just bestowed upon them. His mouth hung open, still hungry as he caught his breath. An unmistakable smile perched on his face as he watched the emotional blow that had been delivered to Ray.

Adrian's eyes never wavered as he glared at Ray, silently challenging him to respond to what he had just witnessed.

I knew the only thing keeping Ray in place was the pearl-handled pistol Lilly had pressed against his back. Her eyes were just as wild as Adrian's and for the first time, I saw how similar the two looked.

Lilly licked her ruby red lips as she brought her mouth to Ray's ear and said, "I know just how you feel." She nodded her head towards her brother and smirked. "His standards always have been low, just like his height."

I wanted to charge her at the moment and deliver the overdue blows she so fully deserved. But the steel firearm reminded me of my inferior position.

"How did you get here, Lil?" Adrian asked, more than a little irritated by their presence.

His beautiful sister scoffed at his question. "What? Were you under the mistaken notion that Samjaza only visited *you* that night in the forest? Did you actually believe you were the only one worthy of his help?"

She nudged Ray with the barrel of the gun, forcing my fiancé to walk further into the tomb. I looked into Ray's eyes and couldn't help but unload my feelings of regret. "Ray, I'm so sorr—"

"Stop!" he shouted. The look on his face surprised me. I couldn't quite grasp what the look was exactly, but it was neither anger nor remorse. "You don't need to explain anything to me, Sid."

He waved his hand and arm in a wide circle, signifying everything around us. "This right here is just a moment in time." He glanced over at Adrian, still very much involved in this silent battle brewing between them. "What you did with him was just a mistake." He spat the word directly towards Adrian. "It didn't define us. And it doesn't define our love, then or now."

All I wanted to do was run into his arms and for a second, I almost forgot about the gun pressed to Ray's back until the tart interrupted our moment.

She looked with disdain at Adrian, eager to get back to her story. "After the disfigurement of my face, thanks to your uncontrollable temper, I had to seek our little friend's help." She shrugged her shoulders. "You left me with no other choice, brother."

"For what price?" Adrian asked as he strode across the room and began searching the empty crypts for something known only to him.

"Patience, dear brother. You will find out the price soon enough." She giggled as she leaned forward and whispered seductively into Ray's ear. "That's going to be the best part. Sit, big boy."

With no other choice, Ray obediently complied, but not without first shooting her a look of loathing.

After ransacking the empty coffin holes against the wall, it seemed Adrian finally found what he was looking for as he reached into the darkness. As I listened to the deafening sound of metal scraping against cement, I was inclined to believe he was revealing the shovel that had damaged my head months before. Could he really have been the perpetrator all along?

I gasped when it finally revealed itself.

Adrian gripped the golden handle of a ruby-encrusted dagger. The same dagger that I'd seen in my dreams. "How is this possible?" I asked aloud.

Adrian rushed to my side. He gripped my face and looked at me the way a parent looks at a young child when they're explaining to them why the sky is blue.

"Your dreams are real, love. You just need to start *believing* them."

I shook my head out of his grasp and took a step back, keeping my distance from him. "This is crazy, Adrian."

He matched my step, refusing to allow any space between us. Then he sent a chill through me. "You can call me Samael."

"And I can call both of you a head shrink if you actually think I'm going to stand by and allow you to live happily ever after," his sister called out.

"What sort of deal did you make with Samjaza?" Adrian asked her.

She smiled, but this time her eyes burned with hatred as she stared at her brother. "How do you think my face healed so flawlessly?"

Adrian pressed her. "What price did you pay?"

She turned the gun towards me, her eyes never leaving Adrian's. "I haven't paid anything . . . *yet*."

"Bygones, sister," Adrian reminded her.

He must have been on the phone with her that night in the library. I remembered him asking a person to forgive and forget whatever history they may have had together.

She exploded in frustration. "You keep saying that, Samael! Let bygones be bygones. I've tried brother, I truly have. But there is only one thing that can fix the unfortunate past."

Lilly nodded towards me. "*She* must go. It was she who contaminated your blood and mind. It was her poison that clouded your judgment and allowed you to inflict such pain on the one person who truly loved you. I do forgive you, brother, because I know without her influence you never would have done such things. She's bewitched you and I shall end the spell she has cast upon you."

Ray's eyes were wide with fear now as he began to climb to his feet. I knew in my heart that he would not let this monster shoot me. He could take her easily. She was just some crazy groupie stalker and he was my big, strong, muscular Ray.

But before he had a chance to do anything, Adrian stood in front of me, acting as a shield, blocking me from his deranged sister.

"Calm down, and start from the beginning, Lil. Tell me everything. How you came here, how you found Ray and Sidney, all of it."

Still waving the gun around like it was a fan on a hot day; she told him her twisted tale. "It was easy, too easy in fact. While Sidney and her Prince Charming were beginning their new life in the City of Angels, I took a little trip myself, up north."

As Lilly spoke this last sentence, she set her catlike eyes on me and waited for my reaction. I had none. I didn't understand a damn thing she was saying.

So . . . she took a road trip up north?

Rolling her eyes, obviously annoyed by my lack of response, she continued. "I wanted to visit an old friend, at least that's what I told Sidney's dear old Granny when I visited that charming little house over on Magnolia Street."

"No!" I cried, as I took a step towards her.

Adrian gripped my arm and pulled me back behind him.

Lilly went on, rather enjoying herself now that she had my full attention. "Your Granny is such a lovely woman, Sidney." Then she frowned as she reflected. "Far too trusting though, she really should work on that."

My heart was pounding. I couldn't believe she'd been inside my house with Granny, while I was with Ray down in L.A.

That rat bitch!

"She invited me in for tea and well, somehow a little bit of methyl iodide must have slipped into her cup." Lilly let out that excoriating giggle of hers again. "Clumsy me, I really should be more careful when I handle that stuff."

I had no idea what methyl iodide was, but it sounded terrible. Lilly put this into my grandmother's tea? Is that what caused her stroke? My Granny was lying on her deathbed because somehow this crazy bitch had a vendetta against *me*.

"Don't worry, lamb, it's not fatal. Once it runs through her system, she'll snap right out of it. I was able to switch her medication the last time I visited her. That overly zealous nurse of hers caught me in her room but I was able to take care of that."

She shrugged as if Nouri was nothing more than an obstacle she had to get around, that her death didn't matter one bit. Tears poured out of my eyes as anger seared from within me. This lunatic had torn apart my life in a matter of months. She killed Nouri, and now she was going to kill me.

"Anyway, I'm sure the doses I've given her have run out by now and so dear old Granny should be waking up any day now."

Holy crap. That means Granny was lucid when she acted like a madwoman today!

"But why?" I asked. "Why hurt my grandmother?"

Lilly stared at me as if I just asked the dumbest question in the world. She slowly responded, enunciating each one of her words, "Because how else would I tear you away from your other half?"

"Stop it, Lil!"

She spewed venom as she mocked her brother, "Oh no, Sam, I'm just getting started. Do you really think you could get Sidney to fall in love with you on your own? I don't think so, brother. You needed my help. The sooner you realize just how much you need me, the easier this will be."

The brother and sister stared each other down, neither one giving an inch.

"So, back to my tale. I do take full credit for Granny's 'stroke,' as the doctors labeled it, which ultimately sent Sidney running back home. Ray, locked into a record deal, couldn't follow, so I preyed upon his vulnerability. What pretty girl wouldn't?"

She shrugged as she glanced down at my fiancé. He was seething, realizing he was nothing more than a pawn in Lilly and Adrian's chess game.

Lilly purred, "He was so sad and alone when I met him. I just had to make him feel better." She brought her hand down to Ray's face and stroked his cheek. "And I did, didn't I, baby?"

Ray slapped her wretched hand. "Get the hell away from me."

"Continuing on, it was my cleverly planned steps that brought us all together. After the old lady fell ill, I was left with limited time to ransack the house and find the necklace Isabel used to wear."

I was surprised how easily she mentioned my mother's name. She said it as if she were mentioning an old friend.

"What does my mom have to do with any of this?"

I was quickly silenced by the barrel of the gun.

"No interrupting!" Lilly screeched.

I burned with desire to know how my mother played into all of this. If only Chrissy hadn't stolen the journal this morning, I could have had time to study those pages instead of being at such a disadvantage.

Funny how even as I stared into the face of death, Chrissy could still frustrate me.

"Your granny is such a pack rat, and because that necklace was buried deep in the attic, it was pretty apparent that she wanted no one to find it. Ever. But I made sure you would discover it by placing it in a box clearly marked with your mother's name on it. All you needed was that pendant and Samael would come for you. The bait was perfect."

She glanced over at Adrian. "You really should be thanking me."

Adrian made an attempt to reason with his sister. "Of course, I appreciate everything you've done, Lil. I really do, but I need you to put down the gun."

Adrian took a step toward his sister, but she wasn't budging. Now she turned the gun in his direction. "I want to remind you of a time, Samael. A time when you chose that little hag over me."

Now the gun was back on me. "I could have given you everything, brother, but you banished me from your life. All because of her!"

She was truly losing her mind.

I looked at Ray and mouthed, "We have to get out of here!" He responded with a slight nod.

"So this is where I get my revenge. *I* am going to banish Eve out of your life. Forever."

All of the color drained from Adrian's face as he gaped in horror. I stood there, baffled. The gun was pointed in my direction, but Lilly said she was going to banish *Eve* from his life, not me.

Surely she was not going to kill *me*.

"Samjaza demanded my blood as a test to you; to see how far you were willing to go to be with your dear, sweet Eve. Would you turn against your own blood and betray your only sister? The only one who stood by your side and loved you in spite of all of your foolish decisions?"

She spat the words directly at me, reiterating the fact that I was his foolish decision. I guess that clarified it, she was planning on killing me.

"Father loved you, Samael. No matter how cruel you may have thought him, you were still his first-born son, the heir to his kingdom. He wanted more for you. Far more than some meager peasant girl. You would have seen that had you not been so stubborn and so blinded by the likes of this inferior being!" she seethed.

Lilly took a deep breath in an attempt to calm herself.

"You passed the test, brother. You didn't kill me. But you didn't leave me whole, either. You ripped my heart out of my chest and crushed every last bit of it before my very eyes. You cut my face because you knew Eve could never possess the beauty that radiated from my being. You attempted to take that from me and leave me with nothing, broken and unwanted."

Adrian exclaimed in frustration, "I did it to save you! I needed to find an escape out of the Garden and find Eve again. Samjaza required your blood, so I merely cut you. Would you rather I have killed you, as he assumed I would?"

Lilly took a deep breath and shook her head, as if she had heard enough and no longer wished to continue this conversation.

"Well, brother, it was a good thing I was not far behind you. I found the Snake and made a deal of my own. He was to repair my face and in return I was to bring him back the soul of Eve."

She took a step towards me and Adrian put his body between us yet again. "No."

She shrugged her milky shoulders. "A debt is a debt."

Adrian gripped the golden handle of the dagger. "I'll never let you hurt her."

Lilly's smile never broke. "Here we stand, brother, in the face of death and betrayal once more." She glanced down at his dagger. "What shall it be this time? A simple slice to my cheek surely won't stop me, that I assure you."

She pulled back the lever on the silver revolver and pointed it at me. I closed my eyes and said a quick prayer. This was it.

Click.

The gun was now cocked and ready to fire.

I suddenly felt sad for the life I would never get to live. I was not going to be a coward. I opened my eyes and stared directly into the barrel of the gun as time stood still.

Lilly announced her final intent. "Life wouldn't be precious if it lasted forever. Goodbye, Eve."

As she began to squeeze the trigger, Adrian lunged forward, knocking her back, which caused the gun to shoot straight up in the air, hitting the cement blocks and sending crumbles of mortar down upon us.

I ducked and shielded my head as the pieces fell, and then I felt Ray's strong arms around me. "Come on, we need to get out of here now."

I took Ray's hand as he led me toward the steps. I still couldn't tear my eyes from the spectacle taking place on the floor of the McAllister mausoleum. Adrian and his sister rolled around, struggling for the gun.

Suddenly, Lilly let out a yelp in pain and became deathly still. Her eyes were wide open as she coughed up a puddle of blood. Her floral print kimono slowly stained deep vermilion. Adrian's ruby-handled dagger was prominently sticking out of her.

Slowly and painfully she forced a smile on her now pale lips. "You still lose, brother. Look at her finger."

And then, Lilly Lavelle took her last breath.

Chapter Nine

I'll Let You Live

It had all happened so quickly I don't think there was any possible way I could have stopped it.

Yet . . .

I played that gruesome scene over and over in my mind and the cinematic picture moved so slowly I had to second-guess myself and believed I *could* have done something to change it.

As soon as Lilly breathed her final words, I attempted to hide my ring finger in my pocket but Ray had had enough of this circus. He firmly gripped my left hand in his and allowed Adrian's eyes to drink in the sight of the large diamond that weighed down my hand.

His eyes shone bright, but these were not the soft emerald eyes of the man whom I'd fallen in love with. These were a fiercely jealous green with a molten fire in them. Burning with rage, they almost looked black. Big, dark eyes contrasting against his porcelain skin.

And now it seemed that all of Lilly's craziness had transferred into Adrian's being.

"You're marrying him?" His words exploded in my face.

I was overwhelmed by the power of his temper, so I shifted my gaze to the floor and stared at the comforting solace of the bricks as I meekly nodded in affirmation.

He softened. "You can't just forget me, Sidney. We were at our best last night. You can't deny that."

I cringed at his response. I had told Ray that I slept with Adrian but I failed to mention it happened just last night, following his proposal.

Ray squeezed my hand, reminding me of his earlier speech. *"Nothing either of us did mattered prior to him placing that ring on my finger."*

My question was, how about *after* he had placed that ring on my finger?

Did that matter?

I looked up at his face and his warm expression confirmed it; Ray was willing to accept me as I was, flaws and all.

Next, I turned my attention back to Adrian. I had to end this madness once and for all, even if it meant accepting the truth, however distorted it may be.

"I know who you are, Samael. I remember you in my dreams. I even love you in them. But the conscious time between my dreams, when I'm awake, I love Ray. I cannot deny that."

With those final words setting in, Adrian turned his full attention towards my fiancé. They both stood, facing off like some scene out of an old western movie when the cowboy kicks open the saloon doors to challenge another to a gunfight at noon. They both stood there, neither one backing down. It was now Ray's turn to shield me, as he stood in front of me to protect me from this crazed lunatic now possessing Adrian's body.

But it wasn't me who needed protection. Adrian was never after me. It was Ray he wanted.

"Adrian, calm down," I said as I jumped around Ray, ready to run to Adrian's side and comfort him, but something told me I shouldn't.

My thoughts were bouncing all over my brain. *I should just stop. Leave him alone. Let him get over me. I shouldn't interfere in his life anymore. It's not fair to him. It's not fair to me.*

"Do you know what it's like to be second best, Sidney?" he replied with another one of his riddles.

Deep in his eyes, I saw the pain behind the rage. There was so much pain. All caused by me. I looked down at the ground in shame. But as I did, I noticed something glisten in the light . . .

It was a blade.

Adrian was still holding onto his dagger. The same dagger he had just used to murder his own sister.

As panic began to set in, I quickly scanned the brick floor in search of the gun Lilly must have dropped during the struggle. I needed it for protection, but just as I spotted it and before I could reach it, Ray lunged towards Adrian, in a valiant attempt to wrestle the knife out of his hand.

That's when pandemonium broke out.

It *seemed* Ray would be able to take Adrian, he was almost a head taller and much more robust, but that wasn't the case. Adrian was just too strong, and before I knew what was happening, he had managed to turn Ray around and had the knife pressed against his throat. He was holding the knife with his right hand, and in his left, he held a fistful of Ray's golden hair.

Adrian held on tight to Ray as he pulled down on his hair causing his head to tilt up and reveal his Adam's apple. All the while, he was staring at me, looking like some kind of wild animal.

I ran across the room and gripped the pearl handle of Lilly's pistol.

"Adrian, stop it!" I yelled as I pointed the gun directly at his head.

I had never shot a gun in my life but I remembered the last time I had set my aim on something; I ended up smacking Ray directly in the eye. I could take Adrian out if I had to. My hands may have been shaking with fear but I knew I would not miss.

Adrian stared back at me, smiling, tilting his head ever so slightly as if he were examining a newborn baby.

"Oh come on, Sidney . . . is this really necessary?"

"Let him go," I ordered, but Adrian did not budge. "Go ahead and shoot me then." He paused, waiting for the bullet that I couldn't bring myself to discharge.

I wasn't a killer. "You can't do it, can you?" Adrian mocked. "Because you love me."

Adrian pointed to me with the knife before placing it back against Ray's throat. "She loves me, Ray. And she's going to let you die rather than kill the man she loves."

I planted both of my feet firmly on the ground as I repositioned the gun and once again, prepared to kill Adrian. But I hesitated.

I closed my eyes and attempted to get a hold of myself and just as I opened them, he did it. In one swift move, he pulled his left hand down and opened Ray's throat.

"Noooooooo!" I shrieked.

My piercing scream must have sent a vibration throughout the universe that was strong enough to shatter the invisible veil that stood between our world and the next, because all of a sudden I was standing in that other world watching myself trying to help Ray.

I watched as the flesh on Ray's neck opened like a zipper and the thick red fluid slowly began to pour out like hot water boiling over. I watched in horror as Adrian let go and Ray slowly dropped to his knees. He didn't even try to stand, he just fell to the ground like a limp doll.

"Don't worry," I heard myself cry. "You're going to be okay."

But my voice was laced with so much uncertainty there was no way anyone would believe me. With that shaky voice, I would be doubted even if I stated that George Washington was our first President.

I was in shock.

But I felt nothing. I couldn't allow myself to be a part of what was taking place. I was alone in that other world. I was only a witness as I watched the actors play out their final scene.

This was not *my* life. This was nothing more than one of my silly little dreams. I closed my eyes and took a deep breath.

"Please wake up," I whispered.

I opened my eyes and all at once I was thrust back into the harsh reality of what was now my world. My own screams pierced my ears as the pain erupted from my chest. This was not a dream, this was reality. My face soaked with tears and my hands drenched in red. All of that blood.

I don't even remember running to him, but there I was, on the ground cradling Ray's head in my lap as his stone cold eyes stared up at me, wide with terror. He was holding his throat while moving his mouth but there was no sound coming from his lips. Just a gurgled gasp as he choked on his own blood.

"It's gonna be okay, Ray. Just hold on," I coached. His blue eyes looked into mine, begging for help but unable to speak.

"I told you that you would choose me." Adrian said triumphantly. "What have you got to say about that, Ray?" he shouted down to my crumbled rock star, kicking him while he was down.

I wrapped both of my hands around his throat in a feeble attempt to stop the blood, but there was just too much. It seeped out through my fingers and wouldn't stay in his body.

"Call an ambulance, please!" I shouted at Adrian before turning my attention back to my fiancé. "Stay with me, Ray. Just hold on, the ambulance will be here soon," I consoled him.

I looked up at Adrian but he just ranted like a madman.

"Call a goddamn ambulance!" I screamed.

Then I heard Adrian's laugh which resonated like a demon from hell. "God won't save him," he proudly boasted. "I beat God. I destroyed his perfect Adam."

And he began to laugh again.

I needed to apply pressure to Ray's injury until help arrived. He was dying.

I ripped off my tan work shirt and crammed it firmly on his throat. Extending both arms, I pressed as hard as I could, but it seemed to make things worse. There was no way to put pressure on the wound without constricting his airway. But if I sat around and did nothing he would bleed out. It was an impossible situation. I needed a needle and thread to close him back up.

I cried out in desperation, "What do I do? What do I do?"

My tan shirt was now a deep purple as it absorbed every ounce of Ray's blood. I wanted to squeeze it and wring it out over Ray, making every drop go back into his open body.

The shirt was useless. The task was beyond my ability. I had no idea how to save him.

Accepting defeat, I slumped my body on top of his and began to sob. "I'm so sorry."

I felt something cold against my cheek and was surprised to see it was Ray's hand. But, it was too cold to be his. He had always felt like sunshine against my skin, and now he felt like a December morning.

I shook my head in denial, unable to accept what was happening. But then I looked at Ray and his face was no longer washed over in fear. He was accepting his fate. He was giving up, which made me freak out even more.

"You need to hold on, Ray. Don't you dare die on me!"

The light in his eyes began to drain out just as quickly as the blood had escaped. I shook my head as I begged him to stay. "Please don't leave me," I whimpered. "We were finally going to be happy."

I said the last line almost to myself. But Ray heard it and he forced his lips to curve into an agonizing smile. They were so pale they didn't seem to belong on his face. His face that always had a natural tan was now as white as snow.

As pale as Adrian.

As pale as death.

And his golden curls were now immersed in a sea of sticky wet red that dominated them. The liquid was mixing in with his hair, dampening it and turning it darker shades that revealed his imminent demise. Ray was preparing to exit this world.

"No!" I yelled, and with a renewed voice of determination, I grabbed the damp shirt and began to press it to his wound again. Ray's eyes never left mine as he struggled to make his mouth move.

"I love you," he lipped.

I knew what he was doing. He was saying goodbye. Before I had time to object, and demand that he continue to fight, it was too late. Ray closed his eyes and didn't open them again. I looked down at Ray—silent, frozen as I waited for those blue eyes I had gazed into since we were kids to open back up. But they wouldn't.

He was gone.

We sat there together in a puddle of his blood as Adrian laughed like a fevered maniac.

I turned and angrily berated him. "What did you do?" I sobbed.

"I did what you didn't have the guts to do. I ended this bullshit! No matter how many times you got burned, you always returned to him, just like a moth to a fucking flame. You were constantly running back to him, depending on him to sustain you, as if he was the oxygen you needed to breathe." His voice mocked me.

He held up his knife like a magic wand. "But I cut that oxygen supply tonight, Sidney. And you're going to find that you *can* breathe on your own without him. You don't need him like you think you do. Now that he's gone you'll see what happiness is. Your vision won't be clouded anymore."

I couldn't believe what was happening.

Ray can't be dead.

I drowned out the nonsense Adrian was babbling as I mourned for Ray. How could I have been so blind, spending my time with a guy who was clearly off his rocker?

I should have known from our talk on the railroad trestle. All of that talk about life and death being a dream. He was a complete fucking lunatic and now he had just killed my fiancé.

Ray couldn't be gone. He just couldn't . . .

I could barely see a thing. Everything seemed to be underwater as I sat on my knees overwhelmed in sorrow. Everything was a blur as my tears tumbled down my face. My sobs were uncontrollable. It was as if Adrian had just ripped my soul out of me. The pain was intolerable.

Adrian's face darkened as he listened to my hysterics. It was as if he truly believed he could just eliminate my fiancé, and with his death, all of my love for Ray would simply evaporate.

He began to have second thoughts now.

"I should have known not to pursue this," he yelled as he paced back and forth in the cold, dark room. Turning, he pointed the dagger at my face. "I told *you* not to pursue it."

There was no point in listening to Adrian, so I turned my focus back on Ray, refusing to give up. "Wake up, Ray," I pleaded.

Denial is a cruel bitch.

Adrian now looked like a caged panther as he foolishly reasoned to himself. "I knew better than this. You weren't ready. Not as long as *he* was still around." Gripping his black hair, he hunched over and brought his elbows to his knees in frustration. "I was so stupid to think that just because I killed him you would forget him. You're too damaged. It's been too long. I took too long to find you. Damn my father."

He dropped the knife and continued to pace back and forth on the cold floor. At that point, my instinct for survival began to kick in and I realized how imperative it was for me to escape.

I calmed myself enough to speak. "Adrian. I don't know what you're talking about."

Collecting my thoughts, I attempted to buy some time. I scanned the room, looking for the fastest way out.

"I told you not to get involved with me unless you were serious. Did you think I was joking, Sidney?" He gripped my shoulders as he shouted directly in my face. "Does it look like I'm fucking *joking?!*"

My mind screamed out, *Oh God, now it's my turn. Now he's going to kill me.*

But my voice was more defiant, "Stop it, Adrian. You're hurting me!"

He let go of me and tried to get a grip on himself. "It shouldn't hurt like this. Love shouldn't hurt this bad, Sidney."

God, he was nuts. How did I not see this before?

Why didn't I listen to those warning bells?

Now I only spoke to survive. "I'm sorry, Adrian. I didn't mean to hurt you," I said as I slowly began to rise to my feet, reluctantly tearing myself away from Ray's lifeless body.

I'll come back for you Ray, I silently promised him. *I won't leave you here.*

Adrian laughed as he shook his head. "You didn't mean to hurt me?" His voice was sarcastic now. "Of course you meant to. What did I really expect, though? Looking for love from a girl who doesn't even know the definition of it. A girl rejected by her own parents left chasing after some loser guy who couldn't give two shits about her," he spat in the direction of my lifeless boyfriend.

I slipped back into the shadows on the cold dark floor, emotionally sinking as low as I had ever been in my life. Nothing he said was surprising; and maybe it shouldn't even be taken seriously coming from a madman. But his words still cut me deep. How could he be so hurtful?

Then, he shifted his emotions again.

He rushed over to the corner and knelt down in front of me full of remorse. The rage slowly faded inside of those emerald irises. But I knew better than to trust this demented excuse for a human being or whatever the hell he was. The lunacy was not gone, it was merely circumvented as Adrian pleaded for me to understand his twisted rationalizations as he attempted to explain away his unspeakable crime. "I-I'm sorry," he stuttered. "I was out of line. I didn't mean to say that."

Out of line?

He just fileted my fiancé's throat and gleefully laughed as he lay dying. But only his words were "out of line"?

He reached out to my face but I swatted his hand away like a disgusting fly. "Don't touch me!"

He took a step back, surprised by my outburst, and so I aggressively took this opportunity to flee. Pushing past him, I made a beeline for the staircase but he was too quick and grabbed my wrist. I ripped my hand away and slapped the side of Adrian's face as hard as I could. He was still in a crouching position and the blow of my hand knocked him completely on his back. Using his moment of vulnerability, I spun around and headed for the marble stairs.

Adrian was not about to give up that easily.

He lunged, face first, across the floor and reached for my ankle, doing everything he could to keep me with him. His grip was so forceful it was like a cement block pulling my entire body to him. My ankle flew backwards as my upper body began to free fall into the darkness.

The last thing I heard was the sound of my head cracking against the marble step. I felt the rush of warm liquid spilling onto the cold floor.

Then, nothing.

Chapter Ten

God Hates Us

I was still in the Garden. It was my last night with Samael and we were desperate to break this curse that was about to be thrust upon us.

I clutched Samael's mother's necklace tightly with one hand as I held my other palm up towards Samael. He brought it to his lips.

"Not a day shall pass without thinking of you, my sweet Eve," he promised.

His words ripped through me, causing a shudder of pain because I knew once I passed through the gates my memories would be ripped away; stolen by his cruel, heartless Father. The thought of my life without Samael seemed unbearable, but a life where I did not remember him was simply not worth living.

"I can't go on without you," I cried. He forced a smile of reassurance on his face but the concern in those green eyes could not be concealed.

"Do not fear, Eve. I shall find you. I will always find you."

He gripped my hand tight and with his other hand, he swiftly slid the sharp blade of the ruby dagger across my palm. He then did the same to his own hand. Together we let our blood drip into the necklace. He snapped the locket shut and placed the chain around my neck. Kissing me, he made me promise once again to never remove the necklace until I grew old and neared my last breath on earth. At that time, I was instructed to pass it down to my next of kin, for the necklace was to be a talisman which would hold our blood, our souls, and our memories. Forever and a day.

Although we both knew better not to trust the wicked man we called the Snake, we had no other option. Samjaza had offered his help at a time when we could not afford to refuse it. Our blood on the necklace was the next of many steps the Snake had in store for us. After our blood was mixed within the necklace we were to take the pendant back to Samjaza and he would place his magic in it. The necklace would forever act as Samael's guide to me.

Again, I began to get second thoughts when I thought of living the rest of my days without the man I loved. "I beg of you, Samael. Do not leave me in this hell forever."

He spoke the same promise. "I shall not rest until I am with you again." *He grabbed my face and kissed me fiercely.* "Now come, we must meet Samjaza tonight and learn of the next task."

* * *

I watched intently as Samael took a nervous breath, attempted to regain his composure, and flashed me his confident smile before knocking on the rickety wooden door.

The old man cracked the door open and peeked his pale gray eye out at Samael and me. As soon as he saw that we had come together, a slick smile spread across his face, revealing his jagged yellow teeth as his eyes darted back and forth between the two of us.

"Ahh . . . the young prince has arrived. And he brought his delicate flower with him," he cackled, waving his long dark hand at us.

It made me nervous the way the Snake was staring at me, probing me with his unsightly, beady eyes. Samael sensed my unease and placed his body in front of mine. I clasped my hands tightly around his shirt, never wanting to let him go.

Samjaza smirked. "We both know very well that your Father would not approve of our meeting."

Samael grew impatient with every passing second that was not being used to enhance our situation. He was not in the mood to listen to the Snake's commentary, and it was causing my lover to shift his weight from one foot to the other.

"My Father is not aware of the everyday activities I occupy myself with, Samjaza. He is not my keeper."

"Oh, on the contrary, my friend," the evil man boasted with a hearty laugh. "Was it not your Father's specific instruction to have Eve banished from the Garden in the first place? After he found out about your indiscretions, or as you put it, everyday activities?"

Now Samael was beyond impatient and I sensed he was a little nervous too as he scanned the surrounding fields, seeking out any possible spies of his Father.

"Will you let us inside or not, Samjaza? I've brought gold and plenty of it," he said in a hushed, but firm whisper.

"Oh foolish boy. You know as well as I it is not gold that I seek."

"I'll do whatever you ask, just let us inside. Now make haste, please!" Samael begged.

The Snake smiled a repulsive smile and opened the door wider. "That's more like it. Come in children, yes . . . by all means, come in."

Samael took my hand as he shoved his way past the Snake and we entered the hut. I could tell by his movements that Samael was becoming more frustrated with every second he spent with Samjaza. Although we were at the Snake's mercy and needed him badly, it did not change the fact Samael still despised the wicked man.

Once inside, Samael began to explain the situation at hand but before he finished his sentence, Samjaza reached out towards my neck and slipped the pendant off. He dipped it in a brew of bubbling red liquid that was roasting over a fire in a cauldron.

"I told you, child, I've been expecting you. There's no need to explain. We all know why you're here."

He began chanting a phrase of Latin words over and over for what seemed like hours. The entire hut was smothered in a massive wave of heat and I wasn't sure how much more I could take of these unbearable conditions. Not only was it hot, but the stench of the dead animals that lined the entire perimeter of the hut made my stomach churn with overwhelming nausea. I glanced over at Samael and I could see he was also suffering in these conditions.

His entire cotton shirt was drenched in sweat and his black hair was matted across his forehead. Upon seeing my face contorted in discomfort, he began to scan the hut in search of some water but saw no basin in sight.

"My lady is in need of refreshment. She is in distress," *Samael said forcefully.*

The Snake ignored his request as he remained in his place above the boiling cauldron. "The soul is the most powerful source to the body." *His eyes remained shut.* "But without a body the soul cannot live."

More interested in answers than water, both Samael and I stood silently, waiting for the old man to continue. The Snake opened one gray eye and stared directly at Samael. "At least, not without magic."

He walked across the room and swiftly placed the brass chain back around my neck, where it belonged. "The pendant has been enchanted. Eve is ready to make her journey now."

The two men stood and stared at each other for minutes in silence. I could see by the look on my lover's face that he was not convinced concerning the promise the Snake had made about my enchanted necklace.

Finally, Samael said, "Then what . . . how do I find her after she leaves?"

His voice began to rise with each additional question he asked. He was desperate for answers, ironic since he was addressing the biggest liar in the universe.

"Eve's soul will go into the necklace and wait until you are able to find her again and free it," Samjaza explained while shrugging his shoulders, as if it were common knowledge.

Samael put his hand to his face and began stroking his chin as he bent forward. I could see he was trying to remain calm, but the Snake's nonchalant demeanor was getting the better of him.

"And do you think you might discover a way to free me from these forsaken gates?" Samael growled, trying ever so hard to contain his burning fury.

I understood his anger, as I was feeling much of the same. Our time was running out and I was beginning to feel we had just wasted the last hour with an old, impotent fool.

"Of course I can," Samjaza replied with a wave of his bony hand. "But that will be discussed later. Meet me at the gates on the morrow and we will discuss the last step." His gaze crept back to me and a smile stretched across his leathery face. "Make sure you bring the girl."

"And what of payment?" Samael asked as we were both being pushed out of the hut by the tiny cretin.

"That too will be discussed later."

I shot straight up, my breathing heavy and uneven. The dreams were back. And I was no longer a spectator. I had assimilated the identity of Eve. Adrian was right when he told me I was she.

I wiped the sweaty mess of brown hair off my forehead and searched around the dark room. I needed to find Adrian and tell him I remembered his words. I had to inform him the Snake did live up to his word and we could be together again.

But then I remembered who I was and where I was, and more importantly, what he had done. I had awakened from my dream and was now thrown back into the reality of my nightmare. Did it really matter if my dreams were true?

Adrian was *still* a murderer. I couldn't forget or ever forgive that fact.

The mausoleum was dark and empty. I searched the blackness but there was no trace of him.

He was gone.

I crawled over to Ray's broken body. He was still lying in the exact spot I'd left him. Again, I tried to bring him to life, but it was no use.

Dead.

Then I remembered the words Adrian had shouted after he'd killed Ray.

"I destroyed his perfect Adam."

I knew now my dreams were not imaginary, they were real. And in believing them, I accepted the fact that I was Eve and Adrian was Samael. This also gave me hope because Adrian had called Ray, Adam.

Could it be possible that Ray was just as much a part of this absurdity as I was?

Could Ray's soul have woken up someplace . . . in the Garden?

Oh my God.

Chapter Eleven

Seize the Day

Still in a daze from tonight's unspeakable events, I stumbled down the narrow cemetery path towards the exit.

Alone.

As I passed the two large oak trees, I didn't even bother scanning their branches as I normally did in search of any nocturnal creatures. After seeing what I just saw, it was going to take much more than a couple of overweight raccoons to jolt me.

My undershirt was drenched in Ray's blood, and I was freezing. I didn't bother to hide the bloody mess that was my shirt as I trudged down the broken, cracked street and headed back into town.

It was odd to think that just six months prior, Adrian and I had walked this same route together. That had been the first night we met. Ray and I had just begun to spiral out of control and in walked Adrian, with perfect timing. But in hindsight, I guess Adrian had always been there with me, somewhere in the shadows of my life waiting to bring me back into *his* reality. Where we could live as Eve and Samael.

But where was he now?

I finally saw with my own eyes who I was, and now it seemed as though he had disappeared.

I had so many unanswered questions but he had abandoned me.

Somehow I found myself sitting on the cathedral steps of St. Catherine's church. It was pitch black as the sun had set behind the golden hills hours ago. I felt like my soul had faded along with the daylight. It had evolved into darkness and enveloped my entire body in its black, mysterious aura. I felt so empty.

The blackness of the night promised to wash away all the sins of the prior day and allow me to start anew when the morning sun would rise, or so I desperately hoped.

If only that were true. If only we could have a do over of this day.

God, I missed him.

I wrapped my arms tightly across my chest and dropped my head into my shivering lap. All I could think of was Ray all alone inside that dark, dank mausoleum. His shimmery blond hair matted in that thick red fluid, his big sinewy neck, gaping open like a gazelle torn apart by lions.

Adrian was right about that movie we'd watched, but he had the characters confused. Ray wasn't Tom Buchanan; he was Gatsby all along. I'd had my Gatsby all along. Everything Ray did, he had done for me. He had accumulated a small fortune, the accompanying fame so he could marry and provide for me. But I refused to see it. Instead, I wallowed in self-pity and played the role of sad little Sidney who could never figure out how to be happy. I had ruined it all. It turned out I was just as selfish as Daisy and now because of my choices, Ray was dead.

"Sidney, is that you?" a gentle voice called from behind me.

I didn't have to turn around to know who the voice belonged to. "Yes, Father Renley, it's me. I'm sorry, did I disturb you?" I asked as I climbed to my feet, ready to move on and take my loitering somewhere else.

"Not at all, my child." The good priest paused while he looked me over, his face full of concern. "Are you hurt?"

I touched my head where it had smacked against the marble stairs after Adrian had tried to stop me from leaving. There was a trickle of dried red that seemed to run all the way from my hairline to my neck. My clothes were soaked with Ray's blood. I could only imagine what an awful mess I must have appeared to the clergyman.

I looked up at Father Renley to gauge his reaction. He had stopped a good distance away from me, clutching his bible to his chest. He looked as if he may have been looking into the eyes of Satan himself, which at this point he very well could have been.

Or, at least his bride.

The last thought hit me deeply as I realized perhaps all this could have been prevented had I listened to Ray and his family in the first place.

"I still haven't gotten baptized," I blurted out, wide-eyed and crazed.

"There's still time for that, Sidney," the reverend reassured me.

"I don't want to be forsaken, Father Renley. I want to go to heaven."

I'll try to believe. I promise I will.

"Of course, my child, of course."

But Father Renley did not move from his step. I don't think he understood the urgency of my dilemma; I needed to be baptized *now*. It was the only way for me to be saved. "If I'm baptized, then I'm forgiven, right?"

Now the Father showed great lines of concern in his face as he asked for some clarification. "Forgiven for what, Sidney?"

I shook my head. "Something terrible has happened to Ray," I said as calmly as possible.

"I'll call for help right away," he said as he turned and rushed through the heavy wooden doors of the church. I stared at them as I considered following him. But crossing through those doors seemed to be an impossible task for me; they were the doors to salvation. A place and a concept I supposed would never welcome me again.

I took this time to stand up and silently depart as I continued my journey into the cold dark night.

Chapter Twelve

Bury Me in Black

Once I reached the locked door, I realized that I had left my purse and keys back at the mausoleum with Ray. I stood in the shadows on the porch, banging on the front door of Granny's house. It looked like someone had taken the liberty to board up the broken front window.

I continued to pound.

Please be home, Chrissy. Let me inside.

Finally, the door swung open.

Chrissy stood inside the doorway staring at me with a look of indifference. I guess she was still deciding whether or not to be angry with me from our earlier spat.

Then she apparently decided to forgive and forget as she rambled on. "Sidney. Thank God you're okay! I went to take a shower this afternoon and when I got out, the front window was smashed in. Emmy's just fine, but I was totally freaked when I couldn't find you. Speaking of your Granny, I have some epic news about her. I've been calling you all night, why haven't you answered your phone?"

Finally taking a breath, she turned to flick the porch light on. Suddenly seeing me under the light, she let out a shriek. I just stood there on the porch, shivering in the cold, unable to provide the answers I knew Chrissy was burning to know.

"Have you seen Adrian?" I calmly asked.

Chrissy didn't know how to respond to the question or anything else I would have said, for that matter.

All she could do was stare at my blood-stained shirt as she shook her head, "Of course I haven't seen Adrian; even if I had, I would have trouble recognizing him. Have you forgotten that he's your most guarded secret and you refuse to let me meet him?"

I took a step into the house and Chrissy jumped back, afraid to get near the ungodly mess that I was.

"Sidney, you're freaking me out. Today you went crazy telling me that some kind of evil spirit was after you, and then our front window was broken, and now you're covered in . . . what is that?"

I stared at her horror-stricken face. I could feel how dry and bloodshot my eyes were and I wasn't even sure if I had blinked in the last five minutes. "Blood," I answered as I dragged my feet over to the couch. I looked up at her and whispered in a conspiratorial tone. "Ray's blood."

Chrissy stood frozen in the entryway of the front door. "Why is Ray's blood on your shirt?"

"I don't know how to explain it." I said as I remained eerily calm. I gripped my emerald pendant. "It all started with this necklace. When I put it on, it must have summoned someone to me, and Adrian thinks I'm someone else, and I think he might be right."

Snapping out of her reserved conversational style, Chrissy slammed the front door and marched over to me, exclaiming, "That's crazy. You're Sidney Sinclair and I've known you since kindergarten. You're nobody other than that girl. Now tell me, is Ray gonna be okay?"

Finally, my eyes began to work again as I felt them blink a few times. They were so dry. I turned to retrieve some eye drops from my purse but then remembered I had left my purse at the mausoleum.

"Where is Ray?!" I jumped as Chrissy shouted the question into my face.

"He's in the mausoleum. I need to find Adrian."

Chrissy gripped my shoulders and started to scream louder as she shook me back and forth like I was the dice inside of a Yahtzee cup. "Snap out of it, Sidney, and tell me what's happened!"

"Ray's dead," I answered flatly. "Adrian killed him."

I paused as I thought of the best way to explain it to her. "But Adrian is not really Adrian. He's Samael and he's been searching for me for a long time, probably for hundreds of years.

"He couldn't let Ray come between us, so he killed him. But I think Ray may be someone else too, and he might not really be dead. He just went somewhere else. If I could just find Adrian, he could answer my questions."

Chrissy let go of my shoulders and took a few cautious steps back as she brought her hand up to her head and wiped the sweat from her brow. "Okay, Sidney. It sounds like you've been through quite a bit tonight." She nervously scanned the room as she continued to retreat. "I'm just going to get you something to drink. I'll be right back."

I nodded to my best friend and curled onto the couch. I was so exhausted. Something to drink did sound nice. A shower also sounded nice, but I was too spent to move. I closed my eyes and fell into a slumber.

God only knew what kind of dream awaited me now.

Chapter Thirteen

Use the Man

"Ms. Sinclair? Wake up." A vaguely familiar voice brought me back into consciousness.

I opened my eyes and slowly sat up; I must have dozed off on the couch. I searched around for that glass of water Chrissy had promised to bring me, but I didn't see it.

Instead, I was sidetracked by a flashing light that crossed my peripheral vision. I turned my head and glanced out the front window to see the blue and red illuminations of a police car.

I looked over in the direction of the voice that had awakened me and saw that it was Detective Albright's. Chrissy was standing in the dining room with alligator tears rolling down her cheeks.

"What are you doing here, Detective?" I asked.

His expression was pained as he took a step closer to me. "I'm sorry, Ms. Sinclair, but I'm going to have to place you under arrest for the murder of Ray Ryker."

Now Chrissy's tears turned into loud sobs as she gripped the back end of the dining chair to steady herself. I shot my gaze in her direction as I angrily shouted, "I thought you were bringing me some water, not calling the cops on me!"

The detective placed a gentle but firm hand on my shoulder. "I need you to place your hands behind your back."

"I didn't kill him!" I yelled, panic beginning to set in. "It was Adrian, I told you that already, Chrissy. What the fuck?"

Detective Albright firmly placed the handcuffs around my wrists and I couldn't help but wonder if these were the same cuffs Ray's wrists were in months before.

"Please, Detective Albright, you have got to believe me. I have to find Adrian and see where Ray went. He might not be dead!"

The Detective shook his head as his eyes filled with pity. "Sidney, the county coroner is at the crime scene right now, there is no doubt here, Ray Ryker is dead. I'm going to read you your Miranda rights and I caution you, do not speak until you have a lawyer."

I couldn't go to jail. What about Granny? Lilly said that she would be waking up soon.

I looked over at Chrissy and this time, instead of hatred, my eyes were filled with desperation. "What about Granny? Who's going to take care of her if I'm not here?"

Chrissy took a step towards me, but then she must have remembered that I was a murderous animal because then she took two steps back. "That's what I meant to tell you. I think Emmy might be waking up."

Of course she was waking up, just as Lilly had predicted. I exhaled a small sigh of relief. At least, in this horrific series of events, one good thing was certain to come out of it.

Granny will live.

The detective began to lead me out of the house and into the darkness; a familiar place in my life.

I turned to Chrissy with one last request. I suddenly remembered that Adrian had passed his bar exam last month. "Please call Adley and Ayers in Sacramento. I need you to get a hold of Adrian and have him represent me. He's a lawyer, Chrissy."

Chrissy shot me a look of indignation while slowly nodding her head in acknowledgement of my request.

Chapter Fourteen

Come Undone

I sat numbly at the stone cold, steel table.

My arms had goose bumps on my pale flesh that had not seen the sun for two days. The authorities had not provided jackets for jailbirds nor did they bother to turn up the heat. I'm pretty sure these conditions were done on purpose to teach us newbie lawbreakers a lesson and make sure that when we were released we'd never return.

Or, at least for those of us that would eventually have a chance to leave.

Some of us would have to board that white bus and take a one-way trip to our final destination, also known as the penitentiary. After all, I was arrested for murder. I wouldn't be incarcerated in a county jail.

When I was a kid I would hear stories about the vicious girls in "The Pen," and the brutality they imposed on new inmates. I sure hoped these were just tales for my sake.

I shivered at the thought, which had turned my pale flesh into the clone of a plucked chicken. I hoped the women in prison only listened to rap music and had no idea who the hell Ray Ryker was.

So far I hadn't seen another inmate since I'd been here. I was kept in a single cell and taken out for a few minutes in the evening to stretch my legs and walk a short distance with a guard. But even on those walks I never saw another prisoner. I began to wonder if I was being kept in my own private facility. A jail constructed just for me.

Maybe Ray's record label funded it.

In addition to people, I also hadn't seen the sun in days and I desperately missed those warm rays basting my skin. I didn't even feel like the same person these days. I was more like an empty shell of a human being with all of my emotions frozen in time.

It was the only way to make it through all this. I was now in survival mode.

I stared across the table at the empty chair that stood in front of me.

Someone obviously had requested a visit with me today and I could only think of one person. I hadn't heard boo from Chrissy, but I could only hope that she at least honored my last request and called Adrian. It was the least she could do for me after sending me to this God-awful place. I had killed no one. I didn't belong here.

This was the first time I had seen any part of the general population but I was too entwined in my own feelings to care about them now. I scanned the giant room full of visitors looking for that mass of black hair but couldn't seem to find him.

Initially I wasn't quite sure how I felt about him coming here but now as my anxiety began to rise I realized that I did, in fact, want to see him.

I needed to see him.

He was the only person that ever understood me and right now, I didn't even understand myself. Plus, I needed to convince him to tell the truth about what had really happened that night in the mausoleum.

Getting more frantic with every passing second, I stood up and leaned over the table, stretching my neck to get a better view of the crowd.

He has to be here.

My rising panic was interrupted when an older woman wearing a beige dress suit stood in front of the table, coughing loudly to get my attention. "Are you expecting someone, Miss Sinclair?" the woman asked.

She definitely looked as if she was lost; she couldn't possibly be here for me.

But how did she know my name? Our shirts had *numbers* stitched on the front of them, not names.

She had short rusty hair that was worn in tight curls with glasses that matched her tresses. The glasses rested at the tip of her long thin nose as she glanced over them at me. She kind of reminded me of P.L. Travers and I smirked at the thought of the Mary Poppins author visiting me in jail.

She clutched a clipboard with a thick manila folder held close to her thin, frail chest.

"No, I uh . . . w-was just," I stuttered, thinking of something to say that would get her to leave me alone. Instead, she set the folder down on the table and read a name off her clipboard.

"Adrian, maybe? Adrian McAllister. He's your boyfriend, right?"

Now she had my full attention as I slowly turned my eyes towards her, drinking in every detail of this woman. I re-evaluated this intruder with a different perspective now. I knew exactly why she was here. She wasn't lost; she had intentionally come here looking for me. She requested this visit. Not Adrian.

I sat back in the chair and folded my arms across my chest in defiance. I could see right through her pathetic attempts of intimacy. She was obviously reading notes from my personal file pretending to know me.

She knew nothing about me. Nothing about my life. I resented her.

"I'm Dr. Scott," she said, stretching her thin, manicured hand out towards me. I remained as still as a statue, making no attempt at civility. "May I take a seat?"

I shrugged. "I'm sure you'll take it whether I grant you permission or not."

Her tight glossed lips stretched into a smile. "Smart girl," she complimented me as she sat in the empty chair across from me. The seconds stretched into minutes and finally I couldn't take her probing eyes any longer. I decided to break the awkward silence between us. "He is my friend."

"Pardon?"

I swallowed hard. "You asked if I was waiting for my boyfriend, Adrian. He's not my boyfriend. He was just a friend."

With this new piece of information, Dr. Scott opened the thick folder and began scribbling into it. Without looking up from her work, she asked, "Any reason you referred to your friendship with Adrian in the past tense the second time?" she asked.

I blinked at her in confusion.

She set down her pen and stared at me through her thick lenses. "Originally, you said he *is* your friend. The second time you said *was*. Any reason?"

My walls began to rise up again. This strange woman was asking too many questions. And they were too technical. Who cares if I said is or was? Was she trying to psychoanalyze me?

I confronted her. "Why are you here, lady? Who are you?"

"I was appointed by the court to evaluate your mental competency and determine if you can stand trial or not."

"Because they still think I killed Ray," I concluded.

Now the pieces of the puzzle were beginning to fall into place.

"Did you?" she asked.

"Of course not!"

I noticed the doctor had stopped writing in her folder. It kind of bothered me. Shouldn't she be writing that I did not kill Ray? That seemed like a fairly important piece of information.

She had a follow-up question. "Do you know who's responsible?"

I crossed my arms in defiance again. I no longer wanted to speak with Dr. Scott.

"Sidney, I'm not here to judge. Only God can do that. I'm only here to gather the truth."

I was exasperated. "What if there is no God? Who judges us then?" I countered, angry that she would even discuss God. What gave her the right to just assume that I believed that He existed? She had no idea about my religious beliefs or if I found her words offensive. She had no idea how complex things became over the past 48 hours. That it wasn't that simple anymore to just believe or not believe.

I didn't know what to believe anymore.

"You must believe in *some* Higher Power," she pressed, her pen in hand like a loaded gun.

"Adrian told me there was no God. We won't be judged because there's no worse place to go. This is hell."

I gritted through my teeth, stabbing my index finger several times onto the metal table. I looked up to meet her solemn gaze and noticed that my actions must have frightened her a bit, for she was pressed against her chair, keeping a safe distance from me.

"It's why we're all so sad and miserable," I concluded in a softer tone.

"Are you sad and miserable?" she asked as she wrote again. She wrote a lot this time. It was as if she were never going to stop writing. I sat patiently, trying to catch a glimpse of what she was placing on the paper but her notes just looked like chicken scratches to me.

Finally, she stopped writing and looked up at me and repeated a portion of her question. "Are you?"

"Yes, I was. For a long time. But then I met Adrian and we were happy until . . . until . . ."

I couldn't bring myself to say it and so I skipped over the hard part and concluded with mine and Adrian's status. "We were best friends."

"You used past tense again."

I didn't answer her. Instead I concentrated on keeping the dam of tears building up behind my eyes in check. I could feel the oceans of water behind them threatening to pour out.

She pressed me, "Are you still friends with Adrian?"

I shook my head in confusion. "I don't know," I answered, as the tears streamed down my face. "I don't know if I can forgive him. I don't know if I'll even get the chance. I haven't seen him since that night."

She closed her folder and abruptly stood up. "I think that's enough for one day."

"Wait!" I began to stand up but the guard shot me a nasty look, so I sat back down in my chair.

I felt strange. At first I wanted nothing to do with this woman, but now I didn't want her to leave. She was the only one I had spoken to in so long. Nobody verbally engaged in this place, even the guards were ordered to ignore all of my questions. I raised my voice before she left the room, "You said the court sent you here to mentally evaluate me? So they still think I'm guilty?"

"Yes," she answered flatly as she smoothed out the wrinkles from her brown skirt.

"But they also think I might be crazy?"

"They just need to rule out that possibility before they can proceed with a trial. It's a legality issue."

Finally, I just came out with the core of my question, "Do you think I'm crazy?"

"I haven't had enough sessions with you to make that determination this early in the process, Sidney."

"Do you think that I kill—" I still couldn't bring myself to say it. It was like if we didn't speak of it then it never happened.

I rephrased my question. "Do you think I'm guilty?"

"We can discuss this further soon. Can I see you tomorrow, same time?"

I rolled my eyes at her tasteless joke. As if there's anywhere else I can be. I've been in this jail for the last two days and it didn't look like I'd be leaving anytime soon.

But the bars trapping me inside my soul were even worse.

Chapter Fifteen

Personal Jesus

That night, as I lay in my cell, I realized I was actually excited to see Dr. Scott again. I mean, I'd much rather see and speak with Adrian, but at this point, I'd pretty much take anyone I could get.

A visitor is a visitor, I reasoned.

And from the looks of it, I may never see Adrian again. It seemed that he was going to sit back in the shadows and allow me to take the fall for his heinous crime.

It may have seemed crazy that I would even want to see Adrian after what he'd done to my life, but in all honesty I still felt as if I needed him. Maybe those dreams were right after all. Maybe we really were soul mates. But if that were true, then where was he?

He told me he wouldn't leave without me. Of course I freaked out when he told me that but now I was almost willing to accept it. At this point, I would go anywhere Adrian wanted to take me. It had to be better than the alternative, which seemed to be three cement walls and a set of steel bars.

Did I still miss Ray? Of course I did.

But the truth was that Ray was gone and I really didn't feel any different because I had always missed him. There was no difference from him being dead or alive, because either way he was still out of my reach. He was always out of my reach. I was just too stubborn to see it.

But Adrian, on the other hand, I missed terribly. He was always there when I needed him. He was always so easily accessible and ready to understand me. The fact of the matter was that Ray was gone and there was no way to bring him back. No matter how hard I cried, pleaded, or begged. But Adrian is here. Or at least he was.

I began to doze off when I was startled by the sound of keys clanking against metal. I sat up, startled, as I looked to see one of the guards unlocking my cell. Behind him, I saw the familiar face of Detective Albright.

The gate opened and the guard glared at me. "You've got five minutes. Not a minute longer." He turned around and gave the detective a much softer look. "Next time come during visiting hours. I could lose my job over this."

Albright nodded his head. "Thanks again for doing this for me, Gonzalez. I owe you."

The two men shook hands and then Gonzalez left us alone.

I sat in bed, staring at the detective in bewilderment as he greeted me with a warm smile. I couldn't return his smile. It seemed my face no longer knew how to make that expression.

Instead, I just gaped. I was emotionally numb and wondering what Detective Albright was doing here.

"Have you gotten yourself a lawyer yet, Miss Sinclair?"

I shook my head no as I pushed a loose strand of hair back behind my ear. "You heard me ask Chrissy to contact Adrian about an attorney. I'm assuming she didn't since I still haven't heard from him."

Just mentioning my best friend's name was causing my hands to shake with anger. Or, it could have been the lack of pills my body so desperately craved. Whatever the cause, my trembling fingers would not let up as my mind angrily doted on Christine Simpson Kyle, my best friend and most insidious deceiver wrapped into one. I had called her daily but she refused to accept my collect calls.

Adrian was my worst enemy but still a better friend than Chrissy, given the circumstances.

The detective stood silent for a few seconds while he sensed my internal struggle. He seemed to be structuring his next sentence to me, carefully choosing the words he would use to communicate his point. He took a deep breath and began straightening his beige tie. The tie was an inappropriate accessory, being the same color as his shirt, which gave it a sort of washed out and unappealing appearance. In addition, his pants had a couple of coffee stains on them, and I had a feeling that this guy was not married, because if he was, I'm sure his wife would have dressed him better before she let him out of the house.

Men, the clueless gender.

"Are you sure that the firm's name was Adley and Ayers?" he asked. "You're certain that's where your friend Adrian works?"

I nodded my head as I watched intently, trying to read the detective's face. He looked like he knew something I didn't and he was preparing to release a giant secret.

I held my breath in anticipation.

He took a step closer into the room and nodded towards the corner of the bed. "May I?"

I nodded and the detective took a seat. The springs screamed in protest as his weight sunk them down to the floor. He looked extremely tired, as if he hadn't gotten any sleep since my arrest. For a brief moment, I almost stood up and asked if he wanted to take a quick nap while I sat in the corner and wrote Chrissy a telegram or something to jolt her into helping me.

He dropped the bomb. "Your grandmother has been transferred back into the hospital."

I jumped up, wondering what could have happened to Granny. Lilly said that Granny would be snapping out of her daze, so why was she now in the hospital?

"Calm down, Sidney. It's a good thing. Her vitals are back up and the doctors seem to believe that she may be waking up soon. She's in the hospital so they can monitor her and make sure they're by her side when she comes to."

I let out the breath that I was holding. "That's great news. Thanks so much for telling me. Is that why you came here tonight?"

The detective shook his head. "Unfortunately not. After your arrest, Ms. Kyle had to gather all the legal paperwork to get your grandmother situated. While going through them, she found the legal document which had appointed you as your Granny's executor of her will."

The detective stopped speaking and looked at me. It looked as if he may have been gauging my reaction, but I was lost here. I didn't even know Granny needed an executor. I just figured the position was automatically appointed to me since there were no other family members to assume the responsibility.

Realizing I was not going to add any input, he continued. "The document was drawn up by a legal firm in Sacramento. Their name is Adley and Ayers. They apparently have been your grandmother's attorneys for a very long time."

"That's weird," I answered, struggling to understand why Adrian had left out such an important legal detail for me.

"Adley and Ayers specializes in family legal services. In fact, they actually handled the adoption paperwork for you after your mother passed and you went to live with your grandmother."

I didn't know what to think of the new information the detective brought to me. "So, Adrian can't help me because he specializes in family law and not criminal cases?"

The detective held my gaze as he spoke a bit harsher to me. "Adrian cannot help you because he does not work for Adley and Ayers.

I called the law firm and spoke to Charles Adley directly. He confirmed that he does not, and has never had, an Adrian McAllister employed in his office."

That obviously was wrong. Adrian *did* work for Adley and Ayers. He told me so himself.

The detective continued what now seemed to be nothing less of an interrogation. "Don't you think it's a bit of coincidence that you believed your friend to be working for the same firm who had been deeply invested in your intimate family affairs your entire life?"

What was he getting at? I had no idea what legal firm handled my grandmother's business. I was just a teenager too engulfed in my *own* life to worry about adult legal responsibilities.

"I don't understand what you're saying, Detective."

Now, my entire body was shaking and I wished that I had my damn pills, or at the very least, one of Adrian's cigarettes. The best I get in here is one benzo in the morning. Just enough to take the edge away. As if anything could ever take the edge away, after what I've been through.

"Adrian does work for a lawyer's office. It was just a temporary position, though. Maybe that's why he wasn't listed on their employee roster, because he's an outside contractor or something. He has his own firm, a family business back in New Jersey. He was only working here for a short time until he could handle some personal business and then he was going back home."

The detective's gloomy expression did not change as his hard eyes bored into mine. "Sidney. I've spent a lot of time chasing leads in the state of New Jersey trying to track down this Adrian McAllister character. They've all been dead ends. No one but you have seen this guy, I'm beginning to wonder if you made him up."

Now my body was burning up. Up to this moment, the entire time I'd been locked in this cell, I had been freezing. Bone chilling, teeth chattering freezing, and now it felt as if someone had cranked the furnace up full blast. I wiped beads of sweat off of my forehead.

"What?" I exclaimed. "Of course I didn't make him up. Ray's seen him. Ray punched him in his face outside the bar, remember?"

"Ray's not here for me to confirm that story."

I started searching my brain for anyone who could collaborate my story and, as I thought about it, I realized that no one else had ever seen Adrian. He always seemed to leave right before Chrissy ever came into the picture. Even though I had always intended to introduce the two, the time never came.

"Jenna!" I shouted out excitedly.

The detective took out his yellow notepad and got ready to write down his new lead. I repeated my source. "Jenna. She's the bartender at The Watering Hole. The first night I met Adrian, I had Jenna send a drink to him on my behalf. She'll remember. Check with Jenna, she'll tell you that Adrian's real."

The detective scratched some notes on the pad just as Gonzalez approached the cell. "Time's up, my man."

The two men shook hands and the detective promised to check in with me tomorrow to report his progress.

Chapter Sixteen

Paint it Black

The third day in jail began just like the last two. I was awakened at dawn by the freezing temperature of the cold cell as I struggled to keep warm with a single cotton blanket that had been issued to me.

Were the taxpayers that broke that we couldn't afford a thicker blanket?

Finally, I gave up on the concept of any comfortable slumber. I'd gotten up and attempted to start my day. Sleep had turned into my only salvation, and I was saddened I could not escape back into it.

Being awake tormented me as my mind flipped back and forth from the loss of Ray to my abandonment by both Adrian and Chrissy. I wished so hard that I could just close my eyes and allow all of my days to pass in the wistful flashes of my subconscious. It was funny how my dreams formerly served as nothing but a nuisance as they refused to allow me a full night's rest, but now they were my friends, my only escape out of this living hell.

And in those dreams, I had always gotten to see his face again.

I know I shouldn't be thinking of him. It was his fault I was in this situation in the first place. But his absence made everything so much worse.

Where *was* he?

If he really was Samael and I was Eve; how could he leave me?

How could he have spent his entire existence from the beginning of time searching for me and then leave me once he found me?

Especially after he had finally made me believe him.

The meeting between Albright and Jenna did not go as well as I had expected. It turned out she did recall me buying a drink for someone that night at the bar, only her memory of what happened was significantly different than mine.

"Jenna insisted there was no man that fit Adrian's description at the bar that night," the detective stated as he peered down at me. "She confirmed she remembered that night vividly because she was surprised when you had offered to buy a man named Jason, not Adrian, a drink at the bar. She was caught off guard because she didn't think Jason was your type."

"Jason?" I spit the name out of my mouth as if it were poison I was ridding from my body. "I didn't buy Jason a drink. Jason reached over and stole the drink I had bought for Adrian."

Now I was livid as the shaking in my hands began to start back up again. I despised that potbellied man Jason and Chrissy and her ugly tattooed friend Dave for trying to set me up with him.

The detective didn't stop with just one blow. He unleashed wave after wave of them. His next one was a tsunami.

He laid a photograph on my bed. It was a picture of a large, white house with boarded-up windows. The yard had not been tended to and the overgrowth was beginning to climb its way up the large staircase to the red front door. My breath was caught in my throat as I continued to stare at what I was seeing here.

The detective said flatly, "I took this picture yesterday."

I was dumbfounded. "You're lying."

"Sidney, I need the truth from you. Everything you've told me up to now has been inaccurate."

I could hear the strain of impatience in his voice. "As you can see, no one has lived in the McAllister house for years. No one has seen you with this Adrian McAllister person and even you admit that you haven't seen him yourself in days."

"I don't understand what you're suggesting," I gasped, my breathing ragged.

I couldn't tear my eyes from the picture. Strangely enough, it reminded me of the drawing in Adrian's book of the overgrown Garden of Eden. This picture could not be current.

He zeroed in on me. "You claim that Adrian killed Ray, correct?"

Now I began to get irritated. Detective Albright seemed to be interrogating me and I thought he was here because he cared about my well-being. I thought he wanted to help me. Most importantly, I thought he *believed* me.

I stared at him, my eyes now cold and full of mistrust. "I don't claim, Detective, I *know*. I was there and I saw what Adrian did with my own eyes. Adrian killed Ray right after he killed his sister, Lilly Lavelle."

Now the detective didn't bother to mask his frustration as he slammed his hand against his knee in exasperation, "We only found Ray's body. Lilly is another person who seems to be a ghost in this story."

Finally I'd had enough of the detective belittling me. I sat back and crossed my arms, indicating that we were finished here. "A ghost . . . maybe that's what they both are."

Wrapping up our meeting, Detective Albright stuffed his yellow notebook back into the front pocket of his wrinkled button-down shirt and turned to me one last time. "Ghosts or not, someone is going to have to answer for what happened to Ray Ryker up there in that mausoleum."

I didn't care to continue this conversation anymore, as it was apparent that the detective was no longer on my side. I turned my gaze, refusing to look at him as I answered. "Well, it looks like that someone will be me."

I buried my face into my pillow, and I heard the metal gate roll open as the detective's footsteps faded away into the distance.

I had never felt more alone in my life.

I sat in my cell for hours after Detective Albright left. I couldn't believe what had transpired here. None of it made sense. I had been inside of that house hundreds of times, it *was* lived in. The front yard was well-manicured, the windows were cleaned. The structure he had shown me in the photograph was nothing more than a dilapidated building.

It was not Adrian's house.

I felt like I was losing my mind. As if the last six months were nothing but a lie. The detective was basically telling me Adrian wasn't real. Dr. Scott revealed to me that the courts were checking my mental competency.

Maybe I was crazy after all.

Did I *imagine* Adrian?

Would that explain all of my unanswered questions that I had for him?

What about all my dreams and the book that retold them so vividly ... how he had ended up connected to Lilly, Ray's mistress? Adrian's explanation about everything was so intimately complicated to say the least. If I believed his story that would mean I believed in sorcery and magic, and soul-creating and demons and eternal darkness, even possession.

But if I believed the singular explanation of what Detective Albright was suggesting, that would mean a much simpler answer.

I was crazy.

But if Adrian was all in my mind, then *who* killed Ray?

Chapter Seventeen

Bury Me in Smoke

Any feelings of excitement to visit with Dr. Scott quickly dissipated after my meeting with Detective Albright that morning.

When Gonzalez came to retrieve me from my cell, I could barely drag my tired legs into the visiting room. All I wanted to do was go back to sleep. I didn't want to be a part of this world anymore.

"Pick up the pace, Sinclair," the pudgy guard barked. "The doctor has better things to do than wait for you all day."

The verbal insults only made me walk slower. What more could possibly be done to me at this point?

Finally my gaze set upon the well-dressed professional that was seated at the steel visiting table and my emotions began to slightly soften. The doctor's hair was worn in the same style as yesterday but she upped her dress suit to a more daring color . . .

Gray.

She smiled upon meeting my gaze, but I just acknowledged her with a slight nod as I took my seat across from her.

Gonzalez shuffled off to go harass other inmates.

"Did you sleep well?" Doctor Scott leaned forward, her eyebrows furrowed as she looked me up and down. I would almost believe that she genuinely cared for me if I hadn't known better.

I shook my head, still avoiding her eyes.

"Why not?"

I really didn't feel like talking to her today, but it didn't seem I had much of a choice in the matter. I was at their mercy now. Sadly, I was no longer a person with the privilege of options.

I let out a loud sigh and answered honestly, "The dreams."

I shifted uneasily in my seat, trying to gauge her reaction before continuing. She wore her poker face well. "They keep me awake."

Pressing the top of her pen in preparation to write, she asked for clarification. "What kind of dreams?"

I shrugged.

Did it really matter what kind of dreams?

She had asked me what had kept me awake at night and I answered her question. Why couldn't we just leave it at that? Growing agitated by her persistence, I answered shortly, "The kind that repeat themselves."

"How long have you been experiencing them?"

I shrugged again. I had hoped she would have taken a hint that I really didn't care to discuss them.

No such luck.

Dr. Scott peered over her glasses at me, serving notice that she did not intend on going anywhere until I began to dish it out. I sat back and crossed my arms. "I don't know. A long time."

I could be stubborn, too.

Opening the familiar manila folder, Dr. Scott began examining the pages, obviously wanting to ask more but getting her facts straight first. I rolled my eyes as I thought that this woman should have done her homework *before* coming here today.

"Before your relationship with Ray began to disintegrate?"

I flinched at the use of his name as well as her choice of verb she had chosen to describe our relationship.

"I suppose," I answered, in a barely audible voice.

Aware that she'd rattled me, she tried a different approach. "What was the main focus of these dreams?"

"Love, I guess."

Scribbling away just as ferociously as the day before, she continued her questions without as much as a glance in my direction. "Are they about you and Ray? Perhaps that was your subconscious looking for other ways to work out your differences?"

There it was again, that unwavering speculation that Ray and I were so terrible for each other.

"The dreams had nothing to do with Ray," I shot back.

She heard something edgy in my answer. She stopped writing and looked up at me intently as she tried to read my body language. I remained frozen in place, not allowing her to see anything.

"You seem tense, Sidney, is this conversation upsetting you?"

What the hell did she think? She came in here with her fancy clothes, scribbling secret notes in her pad, and pretended to know all about my and Ray's intimacy. Of course this conversation was upsetting me. How dare she even speak Ray's name. She didn't even know him.

"You know nothing," I said furiously.

She placed her pen down on the table. "That's a fair statement. I only know what I've read in your file and what I've seen in the media. I'm hoping you will fill in the rest of the details for me."

I snorted at her weak attempt to make us allies.

She was like Russia, and this was the new Cold War. We could never work together.

"Yeah, like I confided in my best friend Chrissy? That's what got me here in the first place."

Now, in addition to being angry at the doctor I was also angry at myself for becoming emotional and discussing the betrayal of my best friend. I quickly placed my hands over my face so she couldn't watch me unravel.

"I understand that you don't trust me, Sidney, but please believe that I am here to help you, not judge you."

I removed my hands from my face and stared at her until she was the one who became uncomfortable. I snarled, "Because that's God's job, right?"

I questioned her with a tone of sarcasm. "Isn't that what you told me yesterday when you came in here and attempted to throw your beliefs onto me?"

She didn't waver at my cruelty. "My religious beliefs are irrelevant."

I let out a dry laugh and almost shocked myself at how much I now sounded like Adrian. But I was on a roll, and I refused to stop. "So, you want me to trust you, but you don't want to share any of your personal beliefs?"

She took the bait. "Okay, Sidney, I'll answer your questions if you answer mine."

I sat back in the metal chair and waited for her to fire away.

She shot straight for the heart. "Tell me about your dreams."

I kept the mask on my face as I gave the most minimalistic answer possible. "They're a story of a man and woman who are in love."

"But it's not you and Ray?"

"The characters were strangers to me. My turn now; do you believe in God?"

The doctor shifted in her seat, and she nervously scanned her notebook in front of her. It almost seemed as if she were looking for an employee handbook which could guide her through my personal questions. "I believe in a higher power, yes."

She smiled tightly, almost proud of herself that she was able to get through my first question. Then she continued her interrogation. "You said the characters *were* strangers to you. Has that changed?"

Well, she did say she was here to psychologically evaluate me. If ever there was a time to not hide my crazy, I guess that time would be now.

I looked up into her eyes and answered truthfully, "Yes, I've met them. It turns out that the woman was *me* in a past life."

I rewarded my answer with a question of my own. "Do you believe in past lives?"

Dr. Scott began to write her notes again. As her hand moved feverishly across the pad of paper she simply answered, "No."

I wasn't satisfied with her response, so I stared at her, waiting for her to elaborate.

She caught on fairly quickly. "I believe that when we die we meet our Maker and that's it. We don't get another chance at life."

I raised my eyebrows at what I perceived to be her pessimistic belief and shrugged my shoulders. "That's a shame."

She ignored my comment and continued her inquisition. "If the woman in your dreams was you, then who was the man?"

I stared at her, waiting for her to say his name. Yesterday she couldn't stop talking about him and today she just sat there pretending he didn't exist. "Adrian." I said it as if it should be common knowledge.

"Your boyfriend?"

"Ray was my boyfriend," I clarified for the hundredth time.

"So then why were you dreaming about Adrian?"

I shook my head, no longer wanting to talk, but then I remembered it was my turn to ask the question. "Do you believe in soul mates?"

She seemed genuinely interested in that question as she tilted her head back and pondered the thought. "I believe that two people can share similarities paralleled so close together that it may produce a very strong mutual attraction, yes."

I learned forward and whispered in a hushed tone, "I believe I dreamt about Adrian because he was my soul mate. I loved him before I even knew him. Is that crazy?"

I now had Dr. Scott's full attention because she gripped the pen so tightly in her hand that her fingertips whitened, and still the pen remained suspended, no longer pouring ink onto the pad. "You mean you loved the man that you saw in your dreams?"

I nodded. My eyes still burned into hers as I waited for some words of advice.

Her answer surprised me. "Assuming that you dreamt about a man and then met someone in real life who shared similar qualities to your dream and then fell in love with him, as you put it, that could be understood. It's the same phenomena as when a television viewer develops an attraction for an actor they watch on TV yet have never met in real life. You fall for the fictional character that the actor has portrayed."

I nodded at her example as her words took my mind back into my own fictional world. "Like Mr. Gatsby."

The scribbling picked back up. "That's an interesting selection. Why do you believe you were attracted to a character like Jay Gatsby?"

"Because he would do anything for Daisy."

"He ended up dying for Daisy," she said flatly.

I could see where she was trying to take this. Gatsby was played by Leonardo DiCaprio in the latest film adaptation. He was a handsome man with blond hair and blue eyes. A fact not lost on Dr. Scott. "He held a resemblance to Ray."

Automatically I shut down. My body couldn't handle any more of this torture. "I don't want to talk about Gatsby."

Thinking about the movie and realizing how easily I imagined Adrian was my Gatsby upset me a great deal, because just like Daisy,

I was too stupid to make the right choice. And because of my decisions, Ray was dead.

Somehow for the second day in a row, Dr. Scott managed to break the dam and release my avalanche of tears. And there was a mountain of sadness that came along with it.

She sat still, allowing me these moments of emotion. And when it seemed I was out of tears, she began to cut into me some more, from a different angle this time.

"I understand that Detective Albright has been visiting you."

Wiping my tears, I answered, "I don't want to talk about him, either."

"Did he say something to upset you?"

I didn't take her bait. She knew exactly what Albright did to me.

She waited a while longer before trying a different approach. "Did you disagree with the evidence?"

I laughed at her choice of words. "You call *that* evidence?"

Dr. Scott remained impartial. "I don't find that a laughing matter, Sidney. Your boyfriend was just murdered and the district attorney is anxiously awaiting my diagnosis in hopes of charging you with his murder."

She looked at me long and hard. "This is California and capital punishment is very much an option here since there is a move to bring it back."

I suppressed my bitter humor and returned the doctor's cold gaze. At this point I just didn't care anymore. Dr. Scott and Detective Albright both pretended to care for me, but it was all just a sham. Nobody cared for me. I was alone.

The doctor was relentless today. She was a far cry from the candid but gentler woman she had portrayed yesterday. "The detective has quite a bit of evidence piled up against you, Sidney. The D.A. is very persistent and I think we may be running out of time here."

Now her fake look of concern reappeared on her aging face.

At least one of us was concerned. I wasn't buying in. "That's funny, because I didn't kill Ray. So what kind of evidence can he possibly have?"

The doctor sat back in her metal chair and opened her folder, scanning through stacks of paper that were thick enough to be an encyclopedia. "The police haven't found the murder weapon as of yet but there was a gun with your fingerprints on it."

Then she asked an odd question. "What hand do you write with?"

I glanced at her sideways, "My right hand, why?"

"And what about your friend, Adrian?"

Remembering the night in his library while he was searching for the red book, I remembered watching him scribble a note on his desk. "He's left-handed."

Then the doctor delivered her blow.

It seemed that everyone was full of fatality moves today.

"Ray's injury was inflicted by a blade that cut him from right to left. That's consistent with a person who is right-handed."

Now my head began to spin and my whole body began to shake convulsively. The doctor continued her torture. "In addition, there were only two sets of footprints in that mausoleum. One set belonged to Ray, the other belonged to you."

"No," I moaned.

She persisted to thrust me into a truth that I never would accept. "No one else was in there except for you and Ray."

After shuffling through her stack of papers, she let out a long, exasperated sigh. "The good news for you, Sidney, is that we do have a history of domestic violence here. I would feel comfortable diagnosing you with post-traumatic stress disorder. It's a condition typical for battered women."

The room was spinning and I felt as if I was going to vomit. "I don't understand. Why would you need to say that?"

A look of disbelief washed across her face. "So that you wouldn't be injected with a lethal dose of potassium chloride."

She shut her manila folder and began to collect her belongings. Before departing, she gave it one last shot. "I do believe that you killed your boyfriend, but not with malicious intent. I believe something traumatic happened inside that mausoleum and you acted in self-defense. There were tabloid reports that said you declined Ray's proposal of marriage the night before. Your best friend also reported a fight in which Ray punched a hole in your bedroom wall. You also suffered yet another injury to your head. Perhaps he became physical with you again and this time you defended yourself."

I shook my head in disagreement with her theory. "No. I saw what happened. That's not it."

She scooted her chair back and proceeded to stand up, attempting to reason with me again. "The human brain has a profound way of blocking traumatic experiences from our memories."

"I didn't kill Ray out of self-defense. I told you already that Adrian killed him! Why won't anyone believe me?" I shouted out as the doctor turned and headed toward the exit.

Exasperated, I draped my head across the cool metal table and concentrated on relaxing my breathing. Then I heard the metal chair scoot back, I looked up and saw that Detective Albright had come back for Round Three.

The day just continued to get better and better.

Chapter Eighteen

Nightmare

It appeared Detective Albright had brought goodies with him this time. The first surprise almost made up for his earlier mistreatment to me as he handed me a delectably smelling double cheeseburger from In-N-Out.

I inhaled it.

The next two surprises were well-defined. I had no idea they were coming.

He placed my black laptop computer onto the table and then rested my mother's journal on top of it.

"That's my mother's journal! How did you get it from Chrissy?" I asked.

If I was gracious for the cheeseburger, I was doubly grateful for the detective's consideration of bringing my mother's personal journal to me. I had been desperate to read it and now it seemed I had finally been given a chance to do just that.

I just didn't see the connection between that and my laptop. I wasn't even sure the guards would allow me to keep it. Wouldn't that fall under the category of contraband?

Then the detective clued me in. "Samael is a rather uncommon name, wouldn't you agree?"

I slowly, very cautiously wiped my mouth with the napkin as my mind was reeling, trying to figure out how the detective knew that name.

I guess that's how the laptop came into the picture. He must have read my dream entries.

"So?" I answered.

"Your friend Chrissy explained to me that you haven't yet had a chance to go through your mother's journal."

I nodded in agreement. "That's correct. I was hoping you could leave that with me tonight so that would be possible."

Finally reading it would be a pyrrhic victory at this point. It didn't really matter now. It probably could have helped me back while I was still in the mausoleum, maybe even before. But now, it was going to take much more than my dead mother's thoughts scribbled down in a book to get me out of this mess.

The detective gripped the journal in his hand, making no sign of releasing it into my care. "I've gotten a chance to browse through it."

Now he set down the journal and pointed to my laptop. "I've also had the chance to read some of your documents that had been saved to your computer. It's a pretty big coincidence that both you and your mother wrote about a man named Samael. Wouldn't you agree?"

I placed my hands on top of my forehead and tore my fingers through my hair in frustration; another one of Adrian's traits I must have picked up along the way to losing my mind.

Didn't Lilly mention my mother back in the mausoleum? Something about my mother wearing the *same* emerald pendant? Well, if Adrian's story was true then I guess it would make sense. My mom was cursed with the similar absurdity that surrounded me now. All because of that damned necklace.

Then a very unsettling thought hit me; did Adrian know my mother? Did he have a relationship with her?

No way.

Adrian loved me. *I'm* Eve, not my mother. He loves me and only me.

My mother must have just dreamt about Samael and Eve. The same as I did in the beginning. I doubt she ever met him in real life.

As I was processing all of this conflict in my mind, Albright laid another bomb on me. He tossed the familiar manila envelope onto the metal table. It was the same envelope that Dr. Scott had brought with her during our visits.

It was my personal file. She must have given it to him on her way out. That only proved my theory that the two were obviously working together.

Against me.

"Dr. Scott was able to do me a favor and dig up some old medical records on your mother."

He gripped a sheet of paper and laid it in front of me. "She did not suffer from post-partum depression as you were originally told."

After hearing that sentence a great weight was lifted off my shoulders.

My mother didn't suffer from post-partum depression?

All this time, I secretly harbored the guilt of killing my mother. Post-partum sometimes comes to mothers after childbearing. I believed that my birth was what caused her mental stability to spiral out of control which ultimately caused her to take her own life.

Now Detective Albright was sitting across from me telling me that everything I had ever known about my mother was a lie.

I asked him, "Well, if she didn't suffer from depression, then why did she kill herself?"

"Your mother's condition was much more serious than depression after childbirth." He took a deep breath. "Isabel Sinclair suffered from schizophrenia."

What? My mother was a lunatic. No freaking way.

The detective folded his hands and placed them in his lap as he spoke in a softer tone, "It's a hereditary disease, Sidney, and the symptoms typically do not begin to show until you reach young adulthood."

What was he implying here?

The detective continued his babbling but now the ringing in my ears began to go off as his voice faded into the background. Detective Albright was laying out too much information for me to process. This couldn't be true.

First my mom was writing about Samael, which meant she had the same dreams as I, then she turned out to be a schizo and now Dr. Scott and Detective Albright believe that I have fallen into her genetic steps?

This was too much.

Maybe Adrian's version of things would be easier to handle after all.

If my mother had experienced the same dreams as me, then they really must have been real. That gave me a comforting thought.

I can't be crazy.

But now Albright was suggesting that Dr. Scott prescribe some anti-psychotic medication. "Your visions of Adrian will be suppressed and you will finally begin to see clearly again. You can start to accept the truth of what you've done and we can begin to round up the legal team that you will need to assist you in your trial."

I jumped out of my chair and shouted at the unkempt detective, "I'm not crazy! My mother wasn't crazy either! Just because we could see things that your simple mind can't understand doesn't make us crazy. Samael *is* real. Our dreams were real and Ray's not dead. You're just too stupid to see that there are other worlds than the one we live in."

Now I felt a set of rough hands sink into my rib cage as Gonzalez appeared out of nowhere and snatched me into his grasp. "Let go of me," I shrieked.

But as I began to fight him I only succeeded in getting swallowed up in his blubber. It was as if I was being attacked by Humphrey the Whale.

Detective Albright sat there assimilating all his "evidence," and then stood up.

"I'm not crazy. You know I'm not!" I argued.

Now Gonzalez was dragging me back towards my cell. I watched wild-eyed and helpless as the detective shrank smaller and smaller, watching the big ape drag me out of his sight.

"Girl, you are the definition of crazy. You sliced your boyfriend up and you can't even remember doing it," the intrusive guard said to me as he opened the gates to my cell and threw me in.

I landed on my stomach, feeling the rough floor beneath me, but I didn't bother to get up. Instead I just laid my flushed face onto the cold cement, strangely feeling like Samael must have felt after his father told him his plan to separate him from Eve.

Desperate.

I closed my eyes and begged sleep to come and take me away.

Chapter Nineteen

All Along the Watchtower

The night was halfway through when he gently shook me awake.

I gasped at the sight of him and realized immediately I was both terrified and relieved at the same time. Terrified because the last time I was with him I watched helplessly as he murdered two people in cold blood.

I was relieved because he didn't abandon me like I had initially thought. He had come back for me. He was going to fix this.

I tightly wrapped the thin blanket around myself and whispered, "Adrian, where the hell have you been?"

He shrugged his shoulders and casually answered, "Around."

He remained kneeling in front of my bed wearing that familiar leather jacket and dark denim jeans. I waited for him to elaborate but he remained silent and detached as he stared at me.

I sat up in the bed and wrapped the blanket even tighter around my shoulders to keep my body from shivering. "Around town? Because so far, everyone I've spoken to seems to believe you're a ghost that I've made up."

It was cold in my cell but his presence seemed to make it icy. I could see my breath as I spoke to him in hushed whispers. "I need you to get in contact with Chrissy. She can take you to Detective Albright and get this whole mess straightened out."

Adrian remained still. "I'm not concerned about that right now."

"What?!" I yelled before realizing that my shouting was going to draw attention to ourselves, which brought me to my next question. "How did you get in here?"

He nodded his head towards the cell gate. "Gonzalez let me in."

I rolled my eyes as I silently thought to myself that Gonzalez must have quite the side business allowing guests to sneak in after visiting hours.

Still leaning in front of my bed, Adrian took my hand and held it tightly in his. I attempted to pull away but he wouldn't allow it. "You remember, Sidney. I know you refuse to believe it but the dreams are true. Why else would you be drawn to me? Why else would you choose me over Ray?"

Now I found the strength to tear my hand away from his and once I did, I had to resist the urge not to use my newly-freed hand to slap him across his face for the audacity of his claim. "I never chose you over Ray!"

Adrian argued with a smile, "On the contrary. Ray asked you time and again not to see me but you continued to ignore his requests. Then he asked you to marry him and instead of saying yes, you ran straight to me."

"I *did* say yes to Ray!"

He smiled. "*After* staying the night with me."

Now it felt as if Adrian slapped me with those last words. Slapped me right into silence. I had no clever comeback this time because there was nothing I could say. What he said was true.

Adrian continued to show me the ways of my wrongs. "Then the ultimate choice was laid out in front of you: Ray's life or mine."

Adrian shrugged his shoulders casually. "You chose me because you remembered our lives together, and you love me."

"I chose not to shoot you because I'm not a murderer," I argued.

"No, you chose it because you love me."

I laid my head on my thin pillow and put my hands over my head. This whole conversation was pointless. It didn't matter if I remembered my dreams, my life with Samael, or the fact that I still loved Adrian.

What did any of that matter *now*? My life was pretty much over.

Then I remembered the real issue at hand. "You killed your sister and Ray and now I'm about to go down for it. You also must have done something with Lilly's body because the cops can't seem to find it. They believe she's just another ghost I made up."

I shook my head in frustration. This time as my body shook, I wasn't sure if it was due to my anger or the frigid conditions this place was causing me to suffer.

"They think I'm crazy, Adrian."

Again, my words seemed to have little effect on him. He simply smiled. "They can't find Lil's body because they can't see her. Just like they can't see me."

Oh God, I really am crazy.

Adrian's here with me now, he's actually come back for me but now he's saying the same crap as Albright and Scott. I shook my head in denial as I continued to fight for my sanity. "But Ray could see you."

Then a thought hit me.

It was a question I'd been burning to ask and now I finally had my opportunity. I sat up on my knees and gripped Adrian's shoulders as I stared at him intently. "You referred to Ray as Adam that night in the mausoleum."

Adrian shook my hands from his shoulders. "So?"

"So does that mean he's a part of this too?"

Adrian stood up and began to pace back and forth inside of the cell as his gaze fell to the floor. "I suppose he is. A very small part that's basically irrelevant to us."

Realizing Adrian still saw Ray as competition, I began to accept that he would never give me the answers I sought. I sat back against the wall and crossed my arms. "Ray's irrelevant because you killed him."

"He's not dead."

"Yes, Ray could see me and my sister because he was part of this too. We are all connected."

He struggled with the next line, looking as though he really did not want to share the information with me. "Just because Ray's gone from this world doesn't mean he's gone completely."

I knew it! This was exactly what I was trying to explain to that blockhead detective, but he just wasn't getting it. I was so happy I could jump for joy. "He's back in the Garden, isn't he?"

Adrian cringed at my excitement. But then he creatively constructed his next words to allow me to see how dire the situation could be. "Yes. He and Lil are both back in the Garden."

"Together?" I asked as I felt a new feeling arise; the feeling of jealousy. All of a sudden I wanted to throw up that double cheeseburger I'd eaten for lunch.

Adrian saw his opening and took full advantage of the situation as he fell back into his familiar role of comforting me. "Don't be upset, Sidney. When you dream of the Garden are you ever emotionally wrapped up in Adam?"

"No. I've never even seen Adam in my dreams."

Adrian brought his hand to my face and brushed a loose strand of hair back behind my ear. I didn't flinch as I suspected I might. Instead, I closed my eyes and leaned into his warm palm; allowing the heat of his body to sink into my skin. He still felt so good.

"And what about Samael?" he asked. "How do you feel about *him*?"

Without opening my eyes and without feeling the need to separate the two, I answered honestly, "I told you already. I love you in my dreams."

He gripped the back of my head and pulled me into him.

"Exactly," he whispered into my ear as he gripped a handful of my hair and sharply inhaled. "That's how irrelevant Ray will be to us when we go back. You won't even care if you ever see his face again." He brushed his lips against my cheek. "You'll be too busy being happy with me."

The feeling was a bit unsettling. I couldn't imagine living in the same world as Ray and not loving him as deeply as I do now. But it was time to finally push my selfish feelings aside and worry about what mattered most.

"But will Ray be okay in this other world? He's happy and healthy, right?"

Still troubled by my attachment to my dead fiancé, Adrian answered as best as he could, "Ray's just fine, I promise you."

He reached over and took my hand. "Now can we worry about us please?"

My heart skipped a beat at his words. He still wanted to be with me. But after everything I knew, how could I agree?

I released his hand and scooted back against the wall. "But you're Samael," I reasoned. "You're evil."

He flinched and sounded almost offended. "Says who?"

"It's in your book. You're the devil."

Adrian laughed at my outlandish accusations. "Where does it say that?"

Now he was truly making me feel as if I had indeed lost my mind. Of course I had remembered suspecting Adrian to be Satan after reading those lines in the book but now I seemed to be at a loss for proof as he was now demanding it from me.

I shook my head. "I don't know. It says you're regarded as both good and evil. That you are defined as an accuser, seducer, and destroyer."

Adrian didn't deny it; instead he remained rational. "So how does that translate into me being the devil?"

When asked point-blank, I didn't have a very good answer. "I guess I just assumed it. If I am to believe that your Father is God then you must be . . ."

Adrian grew serious again. "The devil is such a person. But it's not me."

I knew who the evil one was before Adrian had a chance to elaborate. I had seen him in my dreams and had always known who he was. I just never realized *what* he was.

"Samjaza." Just saying the name out loud brought shivers down my spine.

He nodded.

I looked into Adrian's eyes as I attempted to understand all of this. I argued, "But you made a deal with him so that makes you just as terrible."

Adrian gripped my hands firmly as he stared into my eyes. "So did you."

I searched my memory, trying to remember what sort of deal Eve must have made with Samjaza, but realized that I hadn't gotten that far in my dreams. I didn't know what sort of deal Eve had made. Did she sell her soul to the devil to be with Samael? Or was this just his contract?

Adrian seemed so sure we were going to be able to live happily ever after in the Garden. If that were true, then what price did we pay?

As if on cue, Adrian began, "I'm going back home now."

I chose to remain ignorant. "To New Jersey?"

He shook his head as his eyes never left my face. "No, not there. My real home, Sidney; *our* home. I want you to come with me."

How could I go with him? Did he fail to see the three tons of mortar, cement, and the six-inch steel bars that kept me locked in here?

Don't tell me this guy is Houdini.

Then Adrian pulled something out of his back pocket.

Even in the dark I could still see the red rubies glistening magnificently. It was the dagger I had seen so many times before in my dreams. The same dagger he had used to kill Lilly and Ray.

Immediately, I was filled with terror.

"W-What are you going to do with that?" I stammered.

"Stop asking questions when you already know the answer, Sidney." Placing the dagger in my hands he said, "I told you before, this is nothing but a dream. You know what you have to do to wake up from this."

This wasn't making sense to me. "If you wanted me dead, then why didn't you just let Lilly finish me off in the mausoleum?" I asked, more than a little confused.

He looked at me in surprise. "I don't want you dead, Sidney. I want you living the life that was stolen from you, stolen from us."

Again he held the dagger out towards me.

"In addition to the pendant, Samjaza also enchanted this dagger. Had my sister shot you with that gun you just would have been born into another life."

He ran his fingers through his dark hair in frustration. "And having no other descendants to pass the necklace to, Eve's soul would have been lost forever."

It bothered me that Adrian used *her* name instead of mine. I didn't understand the internal battle I was having with myself over a few choice words of his. If Eve and I were one and the same, then why did I feel as if I were competing with her for Adrian's love?

Adrian continued his logic without noticing my struggle. "Whoever's blood touches this blade is allowed access back into the Garden. All we have to do is plunge it into our bodies and when we awake, we'll be in Eden."

His eyes burned bright with passion. They were filled with hope. "We'll be together, Eve."

Saying her name was all it took to undo my commitment here. I broke away from his grip. "I'm not Eve!" I screamed. "And this knife; it's the knife you used to kill Ray."

I shuddered at the memory.

Adrian remained calm, despite my outburst. "The dagger is the only object that can get you back into the Garden."

He was not giving up as he slid the dagger across the floor to me. I didn't give him the satisfaction of my voice, instead I sat in silence, staring at it.

"Life is nothing more than a dream while your soul is sleeping," he persisted.

After a long silence, I snuck a glance in his direction. Our eyes met and the spark that sent the butterflies fluttering inside me was still there. He was still just as beautiful as before and no matter how much I loathed him, I still loved him.

I growled at him, "You and your riddles. I'm sick of them."

He remained calm. "This body means nothing. It will perish in the earth and turn back into dust after you are dead and buried in the ground."

His words sent shivers down my spine.

Why is he talking about me being dead and decaying in the ground?

"I think I know what happens to my body after I die, I learned that in third grade."

The sneer on my face masked any feelings I may have had left for this man. I would never forgive him for what he had done to me. He had destroyed me. He murdered Ray . . .

"I didn't kill Ray," he said, right on cue as if reading my thoughts. "Look, Sidney." He reached across the bed and took my hands in his. I didn't try to pull away this time. It felt too good to have him touch me. So instead, I began to cry. He lifted his finger to my cheek and brushed a tear away. "Why are you crying?"

"I'm crying because I'm so stupid and I'm ashamed of my feelings for you." By now I was inconsolable, heaving as a river of tears rolled off my face. "Why do I still love you?" I whispered.

With that, he took my face in both of his hands and kissed me deeply.

Passionately.

For a second, the walls of the jail fell down and there were no more bars, no more inmates or prison guards. It was just he and I. Everything would be okay if I had him by my side.

He slowly pulled away, opened his eyes, and looked up at me. His green eyes filled with desire.

"You need to understand that all of this is false," he declared, waving his arm across the room. "Almost like an illusion. None of it matters. The only thing that matters is your soul. And it's sleeping right now. Everything here is a dream. Nothing more. Take the dagger and wake your soul up. That's all it takes for us to be together."

He was now pleading with me.

"Remember your own words, Sidney. When conditions are no longer sufficient, we cease to exist. Look around you, Sidney. Conditions are not sufficient."

What he was saying was the perfect solution to all of this. He was convincing me this was one big nightmare that I needed to wake up from forever. I was almost sold on this idea had it not been for all of my grandmother's warnings I had heard growing up. All of the warnings about the devil trying to "steal your soul."

Is that what was happening right now? The devil was the most charming liar in the universe. I had always thought it would be more point blank. Like a little red man with a pitchfork offering me a million dollars and all I would have to do is sign here. Never did I contemplate that the devil would be my gorgeous lover pleading for me to kill myself so we could be together in the afterlife. But then again, wasn't the devil some kind of angel at one point? So it wouldn't be so far-fetched for this beautiful face of an angel to really be the devil trying to lure me from a path of good to evil.

Yes, Satan was that crafty.

I was so confused.

"I want to be with you . . ." I said weakly, unable to lift my eyes to his.

Then it was as if someone flipped a switch and all of a sudden my brain began to work again as the logic came rushing into my head. Dr. Scott had been visiting me daily. There is only *one* reason a psych doctor comes to you while you're in jail.

She believed I was crazy. She had already told me Adrian was not real. That somehow, he was a figment of my imagination. I had refused to believe her. Adrian was as real as this cell. I can touch him, feel him and even love him. But now he's telling me that I need to kill myself and when I do, I'll be reunited with my dead fiancé back in a place where there's nothing but flowers and love and freedom.

Isn't that the exact bullshit I've spent my whole life not believing?

The stories about living your life purely so when you die, you'll go to heaven, and you'll live your happily ever after were being pummeled into my confused mind. Adrian was trying to sell me the same crap that he himself had led me to believe was a sham. He didn't believe in God, or heaven or hell, so how could he tell me to end my life so that we can be reunited together in another land?

But then again if it's wrong, how could I have been dreaming about it? How did my mother dream the same things? Did my mother kill herself to be united with Samael? If so, then why is he now here for me?

Maybe I'm just another soul for him to collect.

Adrian's voice broke my thoughts. "You've been running your whole life, Sidney. You're almost to the finish line." Those green eyes bored into me as he tried to make me understand. "Will you make this one last sprint?"

In a shaky voice, I answered, "I need time to think about this."

"Okay. I'll come back tomorrow night." He leaned in to kiss me. Surprisingly, I gripped his black hair and accepted the kiss, never wanting it to end. The only time I was happy was when I was with him.

Could this really be my life forever if I listen to him?

He slowly broke away, ending our kiss. Ending my salvation. "I love you, Sidney."

And then he was gone.

Chapter Twenty

Wake the Dead

I laid awake until the sun came up, and even then I remained frozen in the same position until the entire day passed and the sun set again. After sixteen straight hours of contemplating, I finally proposed to end my life.

It was the only way to stay with him and to know that Ray would be all right.

Besides, what was keeping me here? I was parentless. After learning what I had done, Granny would disown me just as she had my mother. Ray was dead, and my best friend had betrayed me.

I had nothing to lose by dying.

If there was such a thing as rock bottom, surely I had hit it. The fall was fast, and the impact was brutal. I was in the abyss. I had followed my mother's footsteps faithfully down her pre-destined path of self-destructive craziness. There was no coming out of this. I had dug my devastation too deep to come out of it. I was either going to be stuck in a loony bin for the rest of my life or sit on death row awaiting the same fate Adrian was leading me to follow tonight and forever.

He was right; this was hell. I had spent my entire life searching for a happiness this earth could never provide. We were put here for the sins of our people, so it only made sense that we lived every day as miserable as the previous one. We were all prisoners here, only a few people here on earth ever realize it.

Adrian had helped me see the truth.

Every last human being has been miserable on this planet. If they believed they were happy at the moment, something would inevitably rip away the shallow facade and leave them to wallow in self-pity as they screamed to the skies begging *their* version of God to help them, when really it was He who'd done it to them in the first place.

If I'd learned anything from my time with Adrian, it was the hopeless promise of joy.

As he promised, Adrian arrived that evening. He explained to me that his law firm obtained a court order from the judge requesting to move me to another part of the facility. I knew that Scott and Albright insisted that Adrian was not real and that there was no legal firm representing me, but if that was the case, then how was he present and accounted for now?

It made me smirk seeing him in his fancy lawyer clothes as he arrived at my cell. The Adrian I knew was most comfortable in his denim jeans and Iron Maiden t-shirt. Here, he stood on the other side of the bars that encaged me as if I were a wild beast. He looked handsome yet somehow out of place in his white button-down shirt starched to a crisp as the collar folded down into the black wool vest with his silk, burgundy tie poking out under his vest. His hair looked a little shorter than usual; perhaps it was all the gel holding it captive. I didn't realize how much I had missed him and all I wanted to do was grip that hopeless hair and bring his mouth to mine. But before I had the chance, he entered my cell and placed a set of handcuffs around my wrists.

"We must play the part, Ms. Sinclair," he whispered, flashing me that half smile as he spun me around and led me out into the hallway.

I was now his prisoner and I would gladly accept that role over the one I had become accustomed to. Once out of sight from the guards, we hurried out an emergency exit, which led us down a dark corridor and into the underground parking lot.

I guessed high security wasn't a top priority at the county jail.

"Where are we going?" I asked in a hushed voice as I quickened my pace to keep up with him as we strode across the parking lot, the handcuffs clanking with every step I took.

He opened the door to his old Firebird, and I climbed inside. As I was getting comfortable in my seat he hurried around to the other side and slid behind the wheel. The engine roared to life as he turned the ignition.

"You couldn't have gotten a more discreet car?"

He gave me that self-assured smile of his and leaned over to buckle my seatbelt. His fingers slowly brushed against my stomach, making the butterflies flutter. Reluctantly bringing his hand over to his side of the car, he manually shifted the transmission and the tires squealed loudly on the polished floor of the parking garage.

He laughed. "What does it matter? They're not going to be able to find us in an hour anyway. We'll be long gone by then."

"According to you, we'll be in another world."

He took my handcuffed hands and intertwined his fingers in mine. "I love you, Sidney."

I smiled as my heart warmed. I couldn't believe I had almost let him get away from me. He had searched for me for lifetimes, and I was ready to throw that away. I was so happy the dreams had finally shown me who I really was. Where I really belonged, back in the Garden, with Samael by my side.

I had spent too many sleepless nights pondering over this quest and I knew now I was making the right decision. I was finally focusing on my own happiness instead of worrying about pleasing everyone else.

The drive was quick. He parked on the dark sleepy road under the eucalyptus trees. It seemed like light years had passed since the last time we sat together in this very spot. He reached in his pocket and pulled out a small key, unlocking the steel bracelets on my wrists. He rubbed the deep red lines the cuffs had left in its place. That was my Adrian, always so attentive.

"It's hard to believe it's only been a few months since we first came up here," I said, nodding towards the entrance of the cemetery. "So much has happened since then. This place used to be our haven."

Then, it had become my nightmare.

Once again, I shivered at the memory of Ray's horrific ending.

Adrian brought my sore wrists up to his mouth and softly placed his lips on them as if kissing away all of the harsh mistreatment of the past days; maybe the past months. I closed my eyes and silently believed that Adrian's kisses were in vain. One thousand kisses would never be enough to wash away the heinous events that were forever embedded in my mind.

My only hope for redemption and a new life was the escape to the Garden.

"None of this matters, Sidney. All this world was for us was time spent apart. Are you ready?" he asked, those green eyes flickering with the excitement of a six-year-old boy on his way to Disneyland.

We exited the old car and slowly headed toward the cemetery.

"The dagger's back in the crypt," Adrian explained. "We'll have to go down there and get it."

I clutched his hand tightly as he led the way and I tried desperately to shove the thoughts of Ray out of my mind. But as the cement building that housed the prior generations of McAllister family members came into view, I couldn't help but be reminded of Ray and all we had shared together.

The memorial that surrounded the cement block was huge with candles burning. Flowers and stuffed teddy bears lined the walls all around the mausoleum. It was impossible to look at it and not be overwhelmed with sadness. This was where everything had ended for Ray.

I stopped and dropped my arms to my waist. As much as I fought it, the force was too strong. It was like a giant magnet pulling me to it. No matter how desperately I begged my feet to stop moving they inexplicably disobeyed and led me to the makeshift memorial.

I knelt down in front of a giant handmade poster. A collage of Ray's photographs spread brilliantly throughout the board had covered every square inch of it. I placed my hand on the glossy finish of Ray's face, remembering him as he was in life. He was always so hopeful and passionate about the future. Our future. The same future that was stolen away far too soon.

"You would have turned out exactly like Daisy Buchanan. If you married him, her life would have become yours. You'd be young, rich and gorgeous." Adrian paused for effect. "And incredibly alone. You would be trapped behind the walls of your mansion desperately wanting to be freed. Be thankful I changed that course of your life."

Then, he gripped my arm a little too roughly as he lifted me back to my feet and tore me away from my memories of Ray. We turned in the direction of the mausoleum, but my body would not allow me to go any further.

"What's the matter now?" Adrian asked, with impatience in his voice.

I shook my head as my body trembled. "I can't go down there," I pleaded.

The images began flashing before my mind as I envisioned the bloody scene I was sure awaited me below.

Adrian wrapped himself around me in an attempt to steady my shaking body. His familiar aroma engulfed me as I breathed in his courage I admired so greatly. It felt so good to be in his arms again. It was where I belonged; I just had to remind myself of that. "You're so close, Sidney. You have to be strong. For me. For us."

I took a deep breath and gathered every ounce of strength I had left in my tired body. I reached up and kissed him.

"For us," I repeated.

We crossed the oxidized door, and I realized that I had left one prison to enter another one. Again, I clutched Adrian's hand as we slowly headed down the marble stairs that led to what was once our underground sanctuary. Secluded and hidden from the everyday pressures of life, this used to provide something so much more than what it did now, imminent death.

When we reached the bottom of the stairs, I noticed a glimmer of light in the opening below.

"Is someone down here?" I whispered to Adrian, my body tensing as I prepared to make a mad dash out of there.

I didn't come this far just to be wrangled away by an angry mob of Ray's bloodthirsty fans seeking revenge. I didn't want to think of what would become of me if they actually caught me. I had seen the masses of people standing together outside of the corrections building. Holding their hateful signs and shouting their hurtful words, verbally expressing their abhorrence of me.

Adrian shook his head and squeezed my hand as he continued toward the clearing. We both stopped dead in our tracks as we stood in disbelief, staring into the angelic face of an intruder.

But this was no stranger. I had seen that face a thousand times in the photograph resting on Granny's piano.

This was my mother.

"Mama?" I heard the tiny voice escape my lips.

She was just as beautiful in real life as she was in the picture, with her long, chestnut hair flowing gracefully down her back and her soft brown eyes welcoming and full of love. I wanted to run into her arms and allow her to shelter me from all of the cruel mishaps of this world, but Adrian gripped my hand like a steel vise and I was reminded that I was *his* prisoner now.

I had agreed to that.

"What the hell are you doing here?" Adrian growled through clenched teeth in a voice almost unrecognizable.

My mom's voice was desperate as she turned to me. "I've come to save you, Sidney. You can't listen to him. Don't believe anything he tells you."

I felt the chill of terror shoot through me as I was reminded of the last time I had spoken to my mother. It was in a dream, in this very mausoleum. She had given me the same warning.

Taking me with him, Adrian strode across the cold room and reached into a dark, empty hole which contained the deadly dagger. He let go of my hand and replaced it with the cold object.

His eyes never leaving mine, he instructed, "Remember what we discussed, Sidney? We don't have much time. I'm sure they've already noticed that you've escaped."

"He appeals to your lowest point, Sidney!" my mother shouted, begging me to acknowledge her. I looked at her and then at Adrian, and back at my mother again. I was so confused. Who was telling the truth here?

"Don't look at her, Sidney. Look at me. Focus on us," Adrian demanded.

"When you think the world can't get any worse . . ." she continued.

I ignored Adrian's directive and looked directly into her eyes. I wanted to hear her out. Adrian gripped my face and turned it away from her.

"Shut up!" he yelled at her.

"Then he'll flash that majestic smile, taking form in what your mind defines as pure beauty, masking his true ugliness." She spit in his direction.

"I said shut up!" Adrian fired, his eyes blazing with that same look he wore just days before, on that last day we had been in this crypt with Ray.

"He portrays himself to be your savior but it's a trick, Sidney. He exists only to collect souls and bring them to an even darker being. It's the battle between good and evil. You chose right, my darling girl, when you chose Ray. This demon took that from you."

My head shot up at the sound of Ray's name. I slapped Adrian's hands away from my face and looked at my mother. "How'd you know I chose Ray?" I asked, my eyes filling with tears.

My mother was begging me now. "Don't allow what he's created here to fool you, Sidney. You are here because it's where he wants you to be. Everything terrible that's happened in your life has been because of him. You've given him your heart and he controls what you see. You have to fight him, Sidney. Take back your heart, here and now, or you will die."

I looked at my beautiful, angelic mother, and then at Adrian. The two contrasted so differently at that moment.

My mother, so pure and bright, and Adrian, overcome with his burning rage, was calloused and dark. So unlike the Adrian I had come to love.

Still clutching the dagger, I didn't know what to do.

I loved Adrian and he was offering me an escape out of this chaos. But if what my mother was saying was right, then it meant Adrian was ultimately the cause of all of this confusion.

I wasn't crazy after all. He somehow made it look that way. But even if she's right, how can I be redeemed now?

It was far too late for me. I pressed the knife to my chest. Adrian was staring desperately at me, nodding his head, giving me the approval I needed.

"He's a liar and a beast!" my mother shouted.

And you're a no-good whore!" Adrian fired back at my mother, unleashing all of his fury onto the small, cowering woman.

"Adrian," I exclaimed in disbelief. "She's my mother."

He frantically tried to regain his composure as he ran his fingers through his long, black hair in frustration. He turned and grabbed my arms. Staring deep into my eyes, he pleaded with me. "I can't lose you, Sidney."

"You will not take my daughter's soul!" my mother shouted.

Adrian spun around and lurched toward my mother, taking her throat in his hand and squeezing it as tightly as he could. I screamed for him to stop as I was being reminded of the last time he'd lost control in this very same place.

He looked at her with such hatred, leaving me to wonder how a man who loves me so deeply and passionately could feel so much hatred towards the one who breathed life into me. If what my mother was saying was true then that meant she was once in love with him and he with her. But the way he felt about my mother now was crystal clear. He showed nothing but disdain towards her.

Suddenly an epiphany came to me; would I take her place if I didn't do what Adrian asked?

Perhaps everything had worked for us thus far because I had been subservient. But what would happen if I told him no?

I vividly remembered Ray's fate when I had disobeyed Adrian's request to leave him. What would happen now if I didn't use the dagger to end my own life?

Would he kill my mother in order to teach me a lesson?

Would he kill me?

As if my mother was reading my exact thoughts, she spat at Adrian through gasps of breath.

"You can't kill me, Samael. I made sure of that when I jumped in front of the train."

It was true after all. My mother did know him. Was it his fault she committed suicide all those years before?

"What is she talking about?" I asked Adrian, desperate to learn the truth.

"Don't listen to her, Sidney, she's a liar. She's a crazy, old liar. She jumped in front of that train because she couldn't handle the burden of motherhood. She was a coward, just like your father. They all abandoned you."

He let go of my mother's throat and came back to me, those pleading eyes boring into me. "But I've stayed, Sidney. No matter how hard things have gotten, I'm still here. I'll never leave you. I love you."

My mother cut off his promises. "Just as he asks you now to plunge the dagger into your body, Samael requested the same thing of me twenty years ago."

Her voice took on a deeper sense of urgency. "I told you, Sidney. He takes away what you love most to make you feel empty and alone. I couldn't find the courage to use the dagger on myself but he knew what would make me beg for death."

The tears flowed down her face and the words spilled freely out of her mouth as Adrian glared at her with abject hatred.

She continued. "The loss of a child would send any mother to extreme measures. When he threatened your life—the life of an innocent baby—I saw his real soul. He was pure evil. I knew then why he insisted on me using the dagger. It was a talisman of darkness; an anchor that trapped countless numbers of souls inside. I would never give him what he wanted and so I jumped in front of that train so he could no longer use you as leverage against me. Keeping you safe was all I cared about. You have to believe me when I tell you this."

She took a step towards me but Adrian stepped in between us, once again acting as the barrier standing in the way of what I needed most.

The pure heart of my beloved mother.

He spewed venom at her. "Liar! Even in death she's a bloody liar. Don't listen to her, Sidney. She just wants you to continue suffering here in this hell. She never cared about you."

He grabbed my hand and gently turned the blade so that the pointed end was pressing against my chest. "I care about you, Sidney."

I stared into those emerald eyes once again, looking for the approval on his face to validate that what I was doing was the right thing. "Nobody's loved me as deeply as you, Adrian." I said, as a tear slid down my cheek.

He gently cupped my face in his hands and kissed my forehead.

"I'd do anything for you, Eve." Those beautiful green pendant eyes blazed into mine.

I smiled a wistful smile, remembering our short bit of happiness together on this earth and replied, "I know you will. Goodbye, Samael."

I watched as his face went from confusion into pain and finally into rage as I turned the dagger around and plunged it as deeply as I could into Samael's heart.

I called him Samael because that's who he truly was, in all of his present darkness.

Adrian was fictional, a figment of my imagination made up by Samael. He was the perfect man who never existed in reality.

I watched emotionless as Samael fell to his knees.

I coldly observed the dagger sticking out of his chest glowing bright red, like a hot iron of righteousness, oozing all the life out of his evil essence.

Forever.

I watched as the many different faces that Samael had used flashed before my eyes before engulfing his entire body into an inferno of fire. All those years of lies, charm, and deceit of tricking innocent women, trapping their souls, had literally evaporated.

When the smoke cleared the only thing remaining in space was the dagger.

Then, the dagger lit up again and the flames wrapped around the knife until the weapon itself combusted into another small cloud of smoke, simultaneously emanating an outpouring of yellow light, setting free all the entrapped souls as they made their way into the heavens above.

Strangely enough it reminded me of the classic movie, *A Nightmare on Elm Street*, after Freddy's demise and all of the souls he had taken spilled out of his chest.

Funny, I thought Adrian was my Gatsby but he turned out to be my ghoul.

My mother ran over to me and we embraced in a long, desperate hug that was twenty years overdue.

"How did you know I was telling the truth?" she asked, wiping away her tears.

"It was when he called me Eve. The truth was in the last words he spoke when he said he would do anything for Eve and not Sidney, not *me*."

He never loved me. It was always her.

My mother filled in the details. "He was collecting the souls so that he could be reunited with her. He made a deal with the devil long ago; 1,000 souls for Eve's return."

"So was Eve just as evil as he was?"

My mother walked across the room and touched a small plaque that was nailed to one of the old coffins. It was the same plaque I saw in my dream but was unable to read the name. I wiped away the years of dust and was astonished to read the name "Eve" on the marker.

"I don't think so, Sidney. I believe in the beginning they were both good. Samael would go to great lengths to be reunited with her and in the process he was overcome by his obsessive love for her which led to his evil."

She turned and looked at me with sadness in her eyes. "You would have been the *thousandth* one. He came so close to being reunited with her, that's why he hated me so much. If I had done what he wanted twenty years ago, he already would have been reunited with Eve. He blamed me for his plan failing and promised to pay me back by claiming you. But I could never let him take you, Sidney. I gave my life to protect you."

She broke down and sobbed.

I clutched my mother's waist as I buried my face in her chest and wept with her. "Oh Mama, all this time I thought you had abandoned me. I'm so sorry for the hatred I felt for you growing up. I was just so hurt."

She wrapped her arms around me, stroking my hair. "There, there, Sidney. You can smile again. You know the truth now, and most importantly, you're free. Go now, and live the life you were meant to have."

I looked up at her smiling face and felt lost. "Mama, I'm so afraid . . ."

My mother leaned forward and showered me with all of the kisses that had been stolen from my life as a child. "Close your eyes, Sidney, I'll sing you the song I used to sing you as a baby before putting you down for your nap," she consoled.

I placed my head against her shoulder and was not surprised by my mother's song choice of "Jewel." I closed my eyes and listened to the soft melody coming from my mother's enchanting voice. I had been sung to sleep many times growing up, but the voice had always been Granny's. I'd always enjoyed my grandmother singing to me as a child, but the voice now was something entirely different. I finally had my mother singing me her soft lullaby while cradling me in her arms. As my eyelids got heavier, I slowly drifted into that peaceful state of mind until her dulcet tones faded out and I was unconscious.

Chapter Twenty-One

Vortex

It seemed even with divine intervention, I was still plagued with the dreams. I stood in front of the gates of Eden as I watched a horrific scene unfold before my eyes.

Something must have gone terribly wrong because Samael was kneeling on the ground clutching Eve's limp body in his arms as Samjaza stood over them without any emotion.

"Oh God, what have I done?" Samael shouted in agony. Screaming at his love's lifeless body, he desperately pleaded for her to wake up. His efforts were in vain.

Eve was gone.

Samjaza twisted his snakelike lips into a smile as he answered Samael's calls for help. "She's dead. Do not be saddened though, she died in the name of love."

As he held Eve close to his chest, Samael shouted to the serpent, "I should have known better than to trust your sorcery and listen to a snake like you!"

Samjaza laughed at the man's dramatics as he waved him off. "Calm down, you fool. You truly didn't believe I would give her to you prior to paying your debt, did you?"

Wiping his eyes and attempting to catch his breath, Samael responded, "I told you, I have gold. I'll pay you ten times over if you bring her back to me."

"And I told you it was not gold that I sought."

"Name your price," Samael growled.

"Souls," Samjaza said tersely as he stretched his bony finger out towards Eve's body, "From women who love you just as fiercely as this one did."

The Snake handed him the bloody dagger that had been used moments before to kill Eve.

"You must get them to plunge this same blade into their body in the same way Eve had done, in the name of love. On the thousandth one, just as your victim takes her last breath, the life will leave her, enter into Eve, and you will have your lover back forever."

Another wave of the bony hand as the Snake commanded, "Take her now. The gates have been opened and are now blanketed in a spell. If you pass through them quickly you will be allowed to retain your memories. Take Eve and place her body somewhere safe. You have a lot of work to do, boy."

Samael slowly swept up his lifeless love and began heading towards the gates feeling alone and defeated. He was meant only for Eve, how could he encourage one thousand women to fall in love with him and repeat her fate?

Eve and his circumstances were unique.

With each step he took, he began to understand just how hopeless of a task this would be for him. Eve had perished for no reason. He was never going to be able to bring her back.

"Oh, boy?" the Evil One called out.

Samael stopped, too heartbroken to look back. Knowing that he had his ear, the Snake said, "Do not forget to remove her necklace before laying her to rest. It contains all of her memories. Whoever wears the pendant will become spellbound. They will be consumed with Eve's memories of you. If Eve's love is as true as she claimed it to be, then the one who wears the necklace will desire only you, making your task a little easier."

I lay in bed processing my latest dream.

The dream validated everything my mother had told me. I was nothing more than a soul for Samael. A stepping stone to get to his one true love. I took a deep breath and exhaled as I glanced around the bright room.

Then I realized that I was not in *my* bed.

I was still incredibly drained and disoriented.

Where was I and how did I get here?

In the distance, I heard the soft sounds of mourning doves cooing outside of the bedroom window. The risen sun was blazing as it welcomed me to a new day. Groggy with sleep, I quickly scanned my surroundings, rearranging them into an order that made sense.

The white walls contrasted boldly with the deep mahogany woodwork of the room. The richly hued brown beams going across the vaulted ceilings gave it an illusion of a church cathedral.

I murmured to myself, "*I've been in this house before.*"

The old wooden window was framed with the same mahogany wood and it was covered with a sheer, white curtain that was blowing against the breeze of the summer air. I arose from my bed and tip-toed across the room, peering curiously out the window. The backyard was beautifully landscaped with orange trees which framed the picturesque San Rafael hills.

Mount Washington!

I knew this place was familiar. This was the home in Los Angeles that Ray and I had planned to live in someday.

Just as the pieces of the puzzle began to fall into place I heard the keys of a piano being played from outside of the bedroom. I ran across the room, following the familiar sound of the song that only had one singer.

Could it really be true? Could Ray really be here with me?

My bare feet flew swiftly across the wood floor as my heart began to pound against my chest and the heavy brass pendant and its telltale emerald swung back and forth. I skidded to a stop and removed the cursed piece of jewelry from around my neck and held it like the tail of a dead rat. I noticed the decorative wall grille in the hallway. Quickly, I removed the cover and tossed the necklace inside the dark air vent.

It was exhilarating to finally be rid of it.

As I entered the living room, I was greeted by several familiar faces. I was so happy to see them all and feel their collective warmth. But my eyes only focused on one individual.

He sat on the piano bench pounding away at the keys, humming the beginnings of a song that would eventually become his number one single on the Billboard music chart as he sang the lyric, "*Not kissing you goodbye.*"

I stared at him, not wanting to dwell on anyone or anything else in the universe.

His blond hair splashed golden as the sun shone brightly through the large living room window. His blue eyes looked into mine and he flashed me his bright smile.

"Morning, sunshine," Ray greeted as he patted the bench, inviting me to join him.

I glided across the floor and perched myself next to him, still unable to believe that he was really here. He wrapped his arms around me and excitedly began to tell me about the new song he had been working on.

"I mean, it's still a work in progress. Finn's gonna eventually add some guitar riffs to it to make it a little more rock and roll, but overall I think it's gonna stay a love song," he explained, just as passionately as he always did when he spoke of his music.

"I love it," I said, addressing the entire room, resting my eyes on Ray's guitar player. "Finn, you definitely need to add your guitar and get that working in there."

Finn, sitting on the maroon couch next to Chrissy, smiled and I noticed the two were sitting thigh to thigh. I nodded at her silently, letting her know through the raise of my eyebrows that we needed to talk later. Chrissy returned the smile and for the first time in a long while I saw that she truly looked happy.

She stood up and stretched as I observed her pink tank top and matching pajama bottoms. I realized that she must have stayed over last night. Then I looked at Finn and noticed that he was still in his pajamas too.

I gave Chrissy a look that said, *"Where exactly did you sleep last night?"*

Again, she flashed me that sneaky, yet satisfied smile, and skipped over to me, grabbing my hands. "Well, our soon-to-be Mrs. Ryker." She held up my left hand and for the first time I beheld the beautiful white gold wedding band crafted in a pattern of diamonds and blue sapphires which met one large diamond in the middle.

"We have a very busy day ahead of us. First your baptism, that is if you still want to have that grand Catholic church wedding you've always dreamed of, and then off to eat some cake samples with your bestie."

She said this as she rubbed her stomach and closed her eyes. We both envisioned all the different cakes we would soon be eating. Chrissy always had a major sweet tooth, in both men and desserts.

I laughed at the combined craziness and familiarity of my friends as I remembered my mother's final words to me, *"Go now, and live the life that you were meant to have."*

Then I remembered one of the most important people in my life. Almost too scared to ask, I meekly asked, "Has Granny woken up?"

Chrissy gave me a strange look as if not fully comprehending my question and then answered, "Emmy has been waking up at seven o'clock in the morning like clockwork ever since I've known her. In fact, she's on a plane headed down here now."

As the tears spilled down my cheeks, Ray took my hand in his and asked me, "You're not getting cold feet, are you?"

I smiled and shook my head. "Never. Marrying you is my dream come true."

"Me too," Ray answered.

Then I added, "Just don't die on me like last time."

He gave me the strangest look.

I laughed and said, "Never mind. You'd never believe the crazy dream I had last night!"

As we embraced each other he began to sing the familiar song that I had heard before.

The one that had always made me smile.

About the Author

Cynthia Austin is a multi-published author who lives in Northern California with her husband, two boys, and Sheepadoodle named Chowder. They love all things horror, gothic, and Victorian which prompts her friends to dub them as "The Addams Family."

She is an avid reader who may be slightly obsessed with music. She hears music in a way that she believes the artist intended it to be heard: visually, with a storyline that follows. Listening to the songs by her favorite artists, she was inspired to write her first series titled "The Pendant."

Coming Soon!

CYNTHIA AUSTIN'S

BETWEEN LIFE
The Pendant Series
Book Four

**Sidney beat Adrian McAllister.
So why was he still haunting her dreams?**

Reunited with Ray, she should have been living in blissful matrimony. But to move on, means letting go. And to let go means she has to admit she made up Adrian. That he had been nothing more than a figment of her imagination. But if that were true, then why did she still have his pendant?

Trapped between fact and fiction, Sidney navigates through her new life still trying to hold on to the old.

**But what would happen when her past catches up to her?
Is she going to be able to survive the truth?**

**For more information
visit: www.SpeakingVolumes.us**

Now Available!

CYNTHIA AUSTIN'S
THE PENDANT SERIES
BOOKS 1 – 2

**For more information
visit:** www.SpeakingVolumes.us

Now Available!

JORDAN S. KELLER'S
ASHES OVER AVALON TRILOGY
Books 1 - 3

**For more information
visit:** www.SpeakingVolumes.us

Now Available!

TONI GLICKMAN'S
BITCHES OF FIFTH AVENUE SERIES
Books 1 – 2

For more information visit: www.SpeakingVolumes.us

Now Available!

MARK E. SCOTT'S
A DAY IN THE LIFE SERIES
Books 1 – 3

**For more information
visit: www.SpeakingVolumes.us**

www.ingramcontent.com/pod-product-compliance
Lightning Source LLC
LaVergne TN
LVHW041221080526
838199LV00082B/1369